THE
CHRISTMAS
TEARDROP

Kevin McGann

THE
CHRISTMAS
TEARDROP

Hometown Publishers

Hometown Publishers
www.hometownpublishers.com

© Copyright 2020
Kevin McGann

First Published by Hometown Publishers October 2020.

ISBN: 978-1-7770337-6-7 (Paperback)
ISBN: 978-1-7770337-7-4 (E-book)

Library and Archives Canada (LAC) national library collection.

Cover Design by Kevin McGann.

Dedication

To Mathew, Jessica,
Daphne, and Brendan

To my parents,
Maria and Charles

Acknowledgements

To my family and friends,

for their invaluable contribution

and on-going support.

Thank you.

Chapter 1

"How was Ava?"

"As good as gold," replied Michael managing a smile and standing up to leave.

"Are you leaving, again?" she asked sharply.

"Yeah," he said, surprised by her tone.

Emily let out a long sigh. "Can we talk, please?"

"Sure," replied Michael taking a seat.

"What's wrong?" she asked sitting next to him. "You've been avoiding me like the plague, you take off as soon as I get home, and you hardly say two words to me."

"I'm confused about us," he said candidly. "I just think we need some space."

"Space? As in taking a break, space?" she asked looking for more details.

"I just think we both need to take a step back and reevaluate what we are doing," he said honestly. "We say we're friends, but we've crossed that line on several occasions, and it's not right with you seeing Brad."

"Oh, this is about Brad!" she snapped, her tiredness and irritability getting the better of her.

"I didn't say that," corrected Michael, "this is about you and me. Brad is your concern, not mine."

"My concern, in what way?"

"Well, isn't he your boyfriend?"

"We go on dates."

He gave her an odd look. "Do you date anyone else?"

"No."

"To me, that makes him your boyfriend, and you a couple."

1

"Okay, just to keep this moving along, he's my boyfriend, and we're a couple, and?" she asked impatiently.

He thought for a moment. "Let me try to explain this in the simplest way."

"Oh, because I'm simple!" she said mockingly.

Michael took a deep breath, ignored her response, and continued. "Do you tell Brad everything we do?"

"No, not everything."

"Not everything or none of it?"

"Not everything." In truth Brad knew very little.

"Why not?"

Emily felt like she was being pushed into a corner and didn't want to be trapped there. "Because…" she said hesitantly, not wanting to answer.

"Because…some of the things we do as friends he wouldn't approve of?" suggested Michael.

"I guess."

"Then that's a problem," established Michael. "If we only did what all other friends do, you should be able to tell him everything, right?"

Emily sighed heavily.

"Like I said earlier, we need to take a step back, take a break, and reevaluate."

She knew he was right about stepping over the friendship line and with Brad not knowing. "So, what about us?"

"Us?" he asked confused. "From day one you told me we were friends; we have reminded each other daily we are friends, and you even tell your family and your friends, that we are friends."

"I know what I tell them!" she said sharply.

"Emily, I am your friend, and you have a boyfriend, I shouldn't be holding you in your bed; it has to stop. And you know yourself; that's just one example of us crossing the line, we need to reset our boundaries," explained Michael calmly, "especially if we are going to continue to be just friends." Although deep down in his heart that wasn't what he wanted at all, or the way he truly felt about her.

Emily had been hoping to hear something completely different from him, she had feelings for him, and she thought he did for her. But what he was saying now was the total opposite, and it hurt her, and she wanted to hurt him back. "At least Brad can provide for Ava and me. He can afford to pay for my college, put Ava in a private school, and give us a very comfortable life," she retaliated furiously.

"And, what's your point?" asked Michael, wanting to hear her say it.

"He has a plan. What's your plan, Michael? To continue to write books, hoping one day you may get lucky, and maybe one day get one published. And if not, then what? Move back in with mommy and daddy when your money runs out," she said nastily.

"Money? Is that what's most important in your life, money!" he snapped back. "Is that the answer to all your problems?"

"It's better than working my butt off in a job I don't like, and having a child I don't see at nights," she countered.

"What about doing your editing in January?"

"Who is going to want me to edit their book?" she asked in dismay. "Someone like you, Michael, who can't afford to pay me! Even if your book gets published, who would even know I edited it? No one!"

"Emily, you've changed these last few days," said Michael shaking his head. "Did someone say something to you to make you feel like this? This is not the person I know; this is not who you are."

"Maybe someone opened my eyes to what you can't offer me," she said smirking smugly at him. "Besides, who wants to be with a penniless—" Emily stopped herself, she couldn't believe how far she had taken it.

"Say it," whispered Michael.

"No."

"Say it!" he said looking at her.

"No, I don't want to," she pleaded.

"Say it!" he demanded.

"Please, please stop…I don't want to say it."

"Well, let me say it for you…Penniless writer!" said Michael, distraught and extremely hurt. He looked away from her, slowly took a deep breath, and thought momentarily. He looked at her and took his time with what he had to say next. "Emily, you're right. I can't pay for you to go to college, put Ava in a private school, buy you a condo in the city, or give you a comfortable life. So, I will agree with you there, and say that you're one hundred percent right."

Emily saw the hurt in his eyes and had to look away.

"But what I can offer you is someone who you can talk to about anything, who will listen to you, and will genuinely care about what you have to say…someone who will be honest, sincere, caring, and kind…but most of all, someone who will give you love and support. Because the backbone to any couple, to us being friends, is the unconditional love and support you give to one another in good times, and more importantly, in bad times…Then again, maybe he already has all those things covered, you are a couple and I'm not around when you two are together, so I'm guessing he probably does…Which means it just comes down to you and Ava having a comfortable life." Michael hesitated and looked at her, judging by her silence, he was right. "Emily, I believed in you from the first day we met. The problem is you never believed in yourself…in me…and now in us," he said sadly, then stood, put on his coat, and headed for the door.

Emily realized replying was pointless, the damage had been done and whatever she said he wouldn't believe it anyway, and who could blame him. Instead, she remained silent and let him walk away from her. And as her eyes welled up, she wondered, "What she was doing?"

Michael glanced over at her one last time "Enjoy your money, your comfortable life…I'm sure Brad will be a great husband, a wonderful stepfather, and I wish you all the best, Emily." Then turned around, opened the door, and quietly closed it behind him.

Emily fell to the floor crying…

Chapter 2

Nineteen Days Earlier - Wednesday, November 30

Michael looked up at the stars in the cool winter night and smiled proudly to himself. Nine months and it was finished; his dream had finally come true. No matter what the outcome, he had done it, and what made it more special, is that he had completed it three and a half weeks prior to the December twenty-fourth deadline he had set for himself.

He slowly glanced down from the stars at the snow-covered trees, road, and sidewalk, before picking up his pace and turning onto Main Street. He had no set destination in mind, he was just out for a walk, but several minutes into it, he noticed a bar was open across the street and decided to head in its direction.

Emily put on her coat, walked outside, and as she hastily moved away from the entrance, the cool air felt refreshing against her face. It had been a busy night, and her feet were sore, but she wanted to distance herself as quickly as she could from work and enjoy the little free time she had. She was tired of her job, unfortunately it was a means to an end, and her choices were very limited. As she gazed off into the distance, she caught the silhouette of a man walking towards her.

"Are you closing up?"

"Oh no, I'm just taking a quick break, and getting some fresh air," she replied.

"It's a beautiful night," he said looking up at the sky.

"It is," she replied following his stare. "I always try to come outside whenever I get the chance, which unfortunately isn't too often," she admitted, "in fact this is my first time tonight."

"Busy night?" he asked.

"Most of it," she said looking at him, "it's quiet now, I only have a couple in the corner." She liked his face; there was something about it that she couldn't quite put her finger on it, but something. "We're closing in about thirty minutes, are you coming in?" she asked motioning to the front door.

"I am," replied Michael and followed her inside. As he watched her take off her coat and put it behind the bar, he put his around the back of a bar chair and sat.

"What would you like?"

"Pint of Budweiser," he said, watching her walk over to the tap and pour. She was a beautiful woman with light brown hair, chestnut-colored eyes, and a picture-perfect complexion.

"I'm Emily," she said putting the beer down and reaching out her hand.

"Michael," he said shaking it, "nice to meet you."

"You too," she replied curiously, "I've never seen you here before, are you new in town?"

"No, I grew up in Aurora then moved away. I came back about a year ago."

"I'm guessing you live close?"

"I do," he replied, "about a fifteen-minute walk."

"Oh really, what street?"

"Cedar."

"I live on Spruce, we're practically neighbors," she said with a friendly smile. "Is that where have you been hiding for the last year?" Emily caught herself. "Oh, I'm sorry! That's none of my business."

"No, it's all right," he said with a reassuring gesture. "I've been busy working; long days and late nights."

"So, you're just taking a break tonight?"

"Actually no, I'm done working for a while…well I shouldn't say work, because it isn't work…I mean it is work, but it's fun work," he said trying to explain before hopelessly looking at her. "Am I making any sense?"

"Kind of," she replied, "I'm guessing, it's something you enjoy doing?"

"It is," he said with a satisfactory nod before taking a sip of his beer.

Emily liked his green eyes, his smile, the scruff on his face, and his dark hair. "Do you mind if I ask what it is that you do?"

He gave her a mischievous suspicious look. "I'm not sure if I want you to know the reason why I've been hiding this past year."

Emily giggled at his playfulness. "Okay, okay," she replied, "asking if that is where you've been hiding, was a little too personal. But you did bring up work and that being the reason why," she said leaning forward and out of the corner of her eye noticing the couple in the corner finishing their drinks and excusing herself.

Michael's eyes followed her, and then he watched the couple pay their bill, say goodnight, and leave. "I should let you close up," he suggested as Emily walked back.

"You have time for one more," she replied going behind the bar. "Besides, I still have to clean up a little and do my cash out," she explained, then paused, and leaned on the counter. "Plus, it will also give you some time to decide whether or not you are going to tell me what it is you do."

"Fair enough," he said with a grin before ordering another and paying his bill.

Emily took out the till. "I want be long," she said pleasantly.

Michael watched her go to the office then looked around. He noticed behind him was a good-sized dining room which took up about two thirds of the space, and where he was sitting the remainder, before turning his attention back to his beer.

"I just have to put these chairs up on the bar," Emily explained as she took away his empty glass. When she looked back, she realized he was doing it for her. "Thank you so much, they can weigh a ton this time of night," she said appreciatively, and smiled to herself as she did her final walk around. After she had finished, they put on their coats, and went outside.

Michael waited for Emily to lock the door and turn around. "Are you driving?"

"No," she replied hoping he would walk with her.

"Can I walk you home?"

"I would like that," she replied happily, and walked in silence for a while, until they crossed the street. "Okay, it's decision time?"

"About what?" asked Michael trying to be coy.

"Oh, don't give me that!" she said shaking her head. "You know about what!"

"Okay, okay, enough pressure," he said putting his hands up and surrendering. "I can't take it anymore."

"You haven't seen anything yet, mister!" she said chuckling.

"I'm sure I haven't," he replied and laughed with her.

As they turned the corner onto Maple, she looked over at him. "So?"

Michael slowed down, stopped, and looked at her hesitantly. "Here it is," he said gathering his thoughts momentarily, "for the last nine months I have been writing a contemporary romance novel, and this evening I finished it. So, I decided I would go for a walk, and when I saw your bar was open, to have a celebratory drink."

"That is so amazing!" she said sincerely "I'm so happy for you."

"Thank you," he replied quietly.

"I have to tell you, I'm an avid reader, and I read whenever I can," she revealed. "Maybe one day I'll get to read yours."

Michael looked at her thoughtfully. "Since you've mentioned it, I wouldn't mind having some fresh eyes reading it and eliciting feedback, before I send it off to the publishers," he said tentatively. "Would you be interested?"

"Are you serious? I would love to!" she replied enthusiastically. "Can I?"

"Of course, you can," he replied happy with her eagerness. "I should probably get someone to edit it, too, but that can be expensive. I do have a friend of the family who has a background in editing, and has offered to help, but I'm not sure he's the type of editor I need for this. Then again, my finances are limited, so I may have to take his offer. I guess I'm unsure what to do at this time."

"I can edit it, too!"

"You can?" he asked surprised.

"In college, I used to edit stories for the newspaper, and I also did some work on the side proofreading students' essays to make some extra money. Editing is a passion of mine," she said fondly thinking back. "Now I have to be honest with you, I haven't edited for a while because I never get the opportunity these days, but it's like riding a bike once you learn you never forget."

"Are you sure you don't mind?" he asked.

"Are you kidding? Reading and editing a potential best-seller, that would be incredible," she said excitedly, "and so much fun."

"I can't pay you the going rate," he said nervously, "actually, not even close to it."

"No money," she said adamantly, "I'm happy enough with you giving me the opportunity to do it. These things don't fall on your lap every day, and this is a chance of a lifetime!"

"Okay, you have a deal, editor."

"Thank you, writer," she replied shaking his hand before they continued on their way. "When will you be able to give me a copy?"

"Do you prefer an electronic or a printed one?

"Printed," she replied.

"Then, I will print it tomorrow and drop it off at your work," he said. "That is, if you're working?"

"I am," she confirmed, "eleven till five."

"Then I'll drop it off no later than five."

"Perfect," she said as they turned onto Spruce and happily thought about editing his manuscript. "This is me," she said motioning to her house, "thanks for walking me home."

"It was my pleasure, Emily, and it was very nice meeting you."

"You too, Michael," she replied. "I'll see you tomorrow, before five?"

"Before five," he reconfirmed. "Goodnight."

"Goodnight," she said walking up her driveway, opening the front door, and going inside. As she closed it behind her and leaned on it, Emily realized she was smiling.

Chapter 3

"Is there any way you can watch her for another couple of hours?" Emily pleaded.

"If I could, I would, but I have a dinner date tonight, I'm so sorry."

"It's okay, Brittany, I understand," she said feeling bad for asking her, "I know it's short notice. Can you drop her off here at five?"

"I can."

"Thanks," replied Emily hanging up and turning to the bartender. "Sue, I'm going to have to watch Ava here for a couple of hours. Luckily, I'm on floor so I can keep a close eye on her."

"She'll be fine," replied Sue. "Set her up in one of the booths in the corner, that way I can keep an eye on her, too."

"Thanks, Sue, you're the best."

Michael placed the printed pages inside the two binders, then put them into a bag, and grabbed his coat. As he walked, he watched the gentle falling snow covering the trees, houses, and ground, and it reminded him of a picture on a Christmas card. Arriving at the entrance, a young girl was walking toward him holding the hand of a teenaged girl. After holding the door open for them, he followed them inside, and noticed Emily at the end of the bar.

"Mom!" screamed the young girl running over to hug her.

Michael stood by the door and waited for Emily to finish talking to her daughter, say goodbye to the teenager, before walking over to her.

"I made it," he said cheerfully, "I thought I might have missed you."

"You would've been safe for a couple more hours," stated Emily happy to see him, "one of the girls called in sick, and now I have to cover the dinner rush." Then she looked down at the young girl. "Ava, this is Michael, Michael my daughter Ava."

"Hello, Ava," said Michael with a kind smile.

"Hello, Michael," replied Ava with a big grin.

"The teenage girl who just left was the babysitter and she wasn't able to watch Ava for a couple more hours," explained Emily. "She has a hot dinner date!" She glanced at her daughter and removed her hat. "So, Ava is going to hang out here with me for a while."

"Mom, will you be able to sit with me?"

"For a few minutes here and there," she replied to her daughter's sad expression. "Don't worry, you will have a booth all to yourself and I will get you chicken fingers, a dessert, and you can play on my phone. How does that sound?"

"But Mom, I don't want to sit by myself," she replied glumly.

"I know Ava, but I have to work, it's just for a couple of hours."

"You know Ava," said Michael. "I haven't eaten yet and I'm on my own, maybe we could share a booth, if that's ok with you and your mom?" he asked looking at Ava then Emily.

"Mom can Michael share a booth with me, please?" she begged.

Emily glanced at Ava then Michael. "I don't want to keep you from anything," she replied, "or put you out?"

"Don't worry you're not," he said comfortingly, and then looked down. "Ava, how old are you?"

"I'm eight and a half."

"Well, I have a niece who is eight, her name is Jenny, and I have no idea what to get her for Christmas. Do you think you can help me out?"

"I sure can," she replied glancing over at her mom. "Mom, we are going to need crayons and paper, please."

Emily walked by the hostess area, picked up crayons, paper, and menus then took them to their booth, before going to the bar to order their cokes.

"Who is that?"

"Michael," replied Emily.

"Michael?" asked Sue inquisitively.

"He's a friend."

"A friend," said Sue shaking her head. "I wish I had a friend as handsome as him."

As Ava and Michael ate their food, Emily would stop by once in a while to see how they were doing and noticed the happy smile on her daughter's face. Then she suddenly realized what it was she had seen in Michael's face the first time she met him, kindness.

"I have one last customer to pay me then all I have to do is quickly clean off their table and do my cash out. Which means I'm going to be done in fifteen minutes or so, are you okay till then?"

"Yeah, Mom, we're fine," replied Ava. "I finished my Christmas list for Santa, and Michael has the same one for Jenny," she said passing it to her. "I put my most favorites at the top,"

"Well, that's a long list, let's hope Santa thinks you've been a very good girl," she said looking at it then the one in Michael's hand. "Looks like you have your work cut out for you."

"I do, I'm glad I had Ava's help, otherwise I might have ended up buying Jenny a fire truck!" said Michael making Ava cringe.

"Michael that's for a boy," she said disapprovingly. "Let Jenny know she can thank me later."

"I will," he replied.

"Does she live close?" asked Ava.

"She lives about an hour away," he confirmed, "and she is coming here to visit for the holidays with her two brothers, her mom and dad."

"She has brothers, too. Are they staying with you?"

"They'll be staying with my parents, my place is too small, but my parents do live very close to me and maybe you can meet them."

"I would like that!" she said animatedly.

"Oh, I should go finish up!" said Emily realizing she had been distracted by their conversation. "I will meet you two at the front in fifteen minutes." She left for the bar, and on the way, an older couple waved her to their table.

"Just our bill Emily, please?" asked Linda.

Emily came back and placed it in Tom's outstretched hand.

"We didn't have time to talk today," said Linda, "you've been so busy."

"It was for a while," replied Emily, "thankfully it's died down now."

"How are your parents and sister doing?" queried Linda.

"They're all doing well."

"It's nice to see Ava and Michael having such a good time," she said looking over at them. "You have a beautiful daughter."

"Thank you," she said smiling then realized what else Linda had said. "Do you know Michael?"

"We live right around the corner from his parents. Tom and I are best friends with them, and we've known Michael since he was a toddler."

"Really," said Emily glancing over at him.

"He's turned into a fine young man," said Tom.

"Oh, he's a lovely young man. Kind, patient, polite, and would do anything for anyone," added Linda. "Emily, you remember my daughter, Kristen?"

"Of course."

"Well Kristen and Michael grew up together and went to the same school. There was a group of five of them, thick as thieves they were," explained Linda. "They still get together every so often on a Saturday night and go for a drink. A couple of them are married now, like Kristen, so they bring their spouses along too. You've met Joshua, Kristen's husband?"

"Yes, I have. They were in here not long ago with their two children, Malory, and Noah."

"That's right," said Linda grinning proudly, then something occurred to her. "When Tom and I are away in Florida, or not available to watch the grandchildren, Kristen asks Michael all the time."

"She does?"

"He's excellent with them," she said looking over at Michael as Emily followed her gaze. "But I guess you can already see that for yourself," suggested Linda turning to Emily who was still watching Michael. "One day he will be a great father," she continued as Emily smiled at what she had said, "and a wonderful husband."

Suddenly Emily realized what Linda was saying and looked at her. "I'm sure he will," she replied shyly.

Linda glanced back at Michael and Ava then up at Emily. "If you're ever in a pinch with Ava, Michael could help you out, without question," she said candidly.

"He has a big home-town heart," added Tom, "just like you, Emily."

"Thank you," replied Emily with a shy smile.

Tom grinned back. "Here you go," he said handing her money, "keep the change."

Emily looked down at the fifty-dollar bills. "Oh, this is way too much, let me get you some change."

"No, don't you dare! If you do, I will be offended!" said Tom attempting to look as if he was putting his foot down but coming across as adorable.

"You better listen to him Emily, he's a bear," teased Linda, making them laugh. "Well, we should let you get back to work," she said standing with her husband. "We're just going to go over and say hello to Michael and Ava before we go. Please, let your parents know we were asking after them."

"I will," said Emily as she helped Linda with her coat and watched them walk over to Michael and Ava. She purposely took her time picking up the dirty dishes so she could casually look over and listen to them interact. They talked for several minutes before Michael stood, hugged Linda, then shook Tom's hand.

"Goodnight, Emily," they said walking towards her.

"Goodnight," she replied then took the dirty dishes to the kitchen, did her cash out then stood by the bar next to Sue.

"Emily, you say he is just a friend?" asked Sue, unsure.

"A friend," reconfirmed Emily.

"I've been watching him all night and the way he is with your daughter, he's amazing…and the way you two are together," she said glancing at Emily. "Is there something going on?"

"No," she replied slowly then looked over at him.

"Is he single?" she asked. "I know he isn't married; he has no ring, I looked."

"I don't know if he's single or not," replied Emily as she continued to stare.

"Girl, you're blushing girl," said Sue looking over at her then noticing something in the background. "Oh, look out, coming through the front door, God's gift to women!"

"What?" replied Emily still watching Michael and Ava not fully comprehending what Sue had said.

"There's my angel," said Brad standing next to her, "I received your text saying you're working late. I thought I would swing by, see how you are doing, and pick up Chinese for dinner then meet you back at your place in about thirty minutes."

"What? Why?" asked Emily, confused.

"Oh no, did you forget?" he asked. "I said I wanted to talk to you about something important…you said drop by tonight…I said I would grab some takeout for us for dinner," he explained trying to refresh her memory and giving her a puzzled look.

"That's right…I'm sorry, you did," she said flustered. "It's been a busy night and I've had to watch Ava here, also."

"Don't worry, I understand," replied Brad looking around. "Where is the little Munchkin?"

"She's over there," replied Emily motioning with her head.

"Who is she with?" he asked.

"His name is Michael, he's a friend, and he sat with Ava to keep her company till I finished," she said glancing at Brad. "Do you want to go over with me and say hello?"

"No, I have to get going, I'll see the little Munchkin later," he replied. "Instead, walk me to the door."

When they got there, Brad glanced over at Michael, once he had his attention he turned to Emily and unexpectedly gave her a hug and kiss on the cheek, which she was too late to stop.

"I'll see you soon," he said and left.

Embarrassed, Emily went to the bar to get her coat.

"He is a fine-looking man also," suggested Sue probing, "and wealthy. A girl who catches a guy like that will be set for life and can replace her tired flat waitress shoes for comfortable well-to-do high heels."

"He does have a lot to offer," replied Emily putting on her coat, "but money isn't everything."

"That's true, honey," said Sue, pleased with her friend's response. "You have a good night."

"You too, Sue," said Emily leaving, meeting Ava and Michael at the door, and walking out into the snowy night. "I was expecting to have to rush home for missy here, so I have my car tonight, can we drop you off at home?"

"No, thanks for the offer, it's such a lovely night I think I'll go for a walk before heading home."

"I know what you mean," said Emily wishing she hadn't driven.

Michael looked at Ava. "Thank you for keeping me company, having dinner with me, and your fantastic toy suggestions."

"Thank you for sitting with me and buying me dinner," replied Ava politely, then walked over, and gave him a hug.

"Anytime, Ava," said Michael hugging her back.

"Thanks again Michael, that was very kind of you."

"My pleasure, anytime…Oh, I almost forgot!" he said handing her the bag.

"Is this it?" she asked elatedly.

"It is."

"I can't wait, I'm so excited," she said and was about to give him a hug but caught herself. "Thank you for letting me do this."

"No, thank you, you're the one helping me out."

"I'll contact you and let you know my progress," said Emily, then realized something. "I don't have your cell number?"

"I put it on a sticky note on one of the binders."

"Perfect," she replied, "we will talk soon. Have a pleasant walk and night."

"You too, Emily, and you too, Ava. Goodnight."

"Goodnight, Michael," replied Ava merrily.

Emily held Ava's hand as they walked to the car, jumped in, and started for home.

"I like him," said Ava.

"You do," said Emily. "Why?" she asked curiously, but already knowing her answer.

"He's kind, and he makes me laugh."

"That was nice of you to give him a hug," said Emily, a little surprised she did.

"I wanted to," replied Ava, "besides I think he might have needed one."

"Why do you say that?"

"I don't know, he just looked a little sad before we left."

During the drive home, walking up the driveway, and into the house, Emily had been thinking about what Ava had said, and more so what she had meant by it. But before she could ask her, there was a knock at the door, and Ava left to open it.

Chapter 4

"Hey, Munchkin, how are you doing?"

"Brad, you know I don't like that nickname."

"My apologies Ava, where is your mom?"

"She's in the kitchen."

Emily stuck her head around the corner. "Do you want a beer?"

"No, I have wine to go with the Chinese," he bragged, following her into the kitchen, and proceeding to close the fridge door to stop her from reaching for one.

"Brad, beer and Chinese go together; not wine and Chinese."

"Emily, I paid big bucks for this," he said with a pouty look.

"Okay," she said giving in to him.

"Great, you get the plates, and point me in the direction of the wine glasses."

After they ate, Ava played for a while before Emily put her to bed.

"She's had a busy day," said Emily walking into the living room, "she will be asleep in no time."

"Do you want me to top up your wine?" asked Brad.

"No, I can barely finish this first glass," she said sitting down on the couch next to him. "What did you want to talk about?"

"Well, as you know I have been offered a big promotion, VP of Sales, and I wanted to pick up our conversation where we had left it last time, we met…We talked about you quitting your job, and you and the Munchkin moving with me to the city. A private school for her, lots of travel for you and me, and holidays, sun, and fun for three of us…I was wondering if you had thought about it since?"

"Brad, I don't know," replied Emily hesitantly. "I love it here in Aurora."

"You will love the city, too. It has spas, shopping, and fancy restaurants," he explained, "and our suite will be spacious, with a great view."

"But what about Ava? Her friends?"

"She is young, and she will make new friends," he replied. "You, we, can give her all the things she needs. Plus, the condo has an indoor pool and fitness center, she'll love that."

"I don't know Brad," said Emily shaking her head. "We haven't known each other that long and it's a big decision."

"But we make a great team?"

"Team!" said Emily, not happy with his choice of words.

"You know what I mean," he said quickly correcting himself, "a great couple." He noticed her lack of response and realized his last remark had set him back. "Emily, there is a staff Christmas party in the city this Friday night, come with me and meet the people I work with and their spouses. See what they are like, get a feel for them. Some of them have children, too, you can ask them what it's like raising them in the city."

"I thought you were leaving for a business trip this weekend?"

"I was, I mean I am, but I changed my departure flight to Saturday…I thought this would be good opportunity for us to mingle, meet some people, and have a look around. Maybe help you with your decision and hopefully convince you to move," he said, and then paused momentarily. "The least you can do is give me a chance."

Emily was unsure, confused, and tired. Ava was her priority, so maybe meeting these people was a good idea; they could help her with some questions she had about moving to the city with her daughter. But leaving Aurora, and Ava leaving her friends, her school, and her family behind; she loves it here. Then Emily thought about herself, and what she would be giving up: her best friend Sue, her sister, and her parents. She slowly sipped her wine and went back and forth for several minutes. "Okay, I'll go, but only on a few conditions."

"Name them."

"If I want to leave, we leave."

"Okay."

"I am your date; we are not an item."

"All right."

"Ava and I have a busy day Saturday, and we need to be up early, so I have to be home by twelve."

"That works for me," he replied sounding accommodating, "I have to be at the airport early in the morning. Anything else?"

"No, that's it."

"All right," said Brad with a satisfied grin. "You look tired, I'll let you get to bed."

"Thank you."

Brad finished his wine quickly, stood and put his coat on, then walked to the door. "I'll pick you up around five thirty?"

"That's fine," she replied walking with him.

"Great," he replied, "goodnight."

"Night," she replied, expecting another hug from him. But unlike the bar, there was none this time, and he just left. Emily closed the door, leaned against it, and realized something; she wasn't smiling.

Text to Michael: "Started your novel, love it, can't put it down."

Michael: "Glad you are enjoying it. How's the editing going?"

Emily: "Going good, couple of grammatical errors, some content suggestions…overall it's exceptionally good. Love the story!"

Michael: "Thanks."

Emily: "Getting back to it. Will be in touch."

Michael: "Okay, night."

Emily: "Night."

Chapter 5

"You're sick, oh no, I'm sorry to hear that, Brittany," said Emily thinking for a moment. "Is there anyone else you know who can babysit?"

"You can try Olivia, but I think she might be at a family function tonight."

"Thanks, I hope you are feeling better soon," she said hanging up and looking at the time on her phone, "four o'clock."

"What's wrong, Mom?"

"Brittany is sick," she replied, "I'm going to have to cancel tonight. There's no one else I can get in such short notice."

"What about Michael?" suggested Ava. "He'll watch me for you."

"Oh baby, it's a Friday night, he probably has plans."

"You can still ask him, he did say anytime, and this is anytime, besides I like him, please."

Emily looked at her sad face then remembered what Linda had said, 'if you're ever in a pinch, Michael could help you out.' "I guess I can ask, the worst he can say is, no," she said looking at Ava then dialing his number. "Hello, Michael, it's Emily."

"Hi, Emily, is everything ok?" he asked surprised by her call.

"Well, I have a problem and I was hoping you could help me out?"

"Sure, name it."

"I've been invited to a Christmas party, my babysitter is sick with a cold, and I need someone to watch Ava tonight. I was wondering if you could?"

"What time would you need me there?"

"Around five."

"Okay, I'll be there in an hour."

"Are you sure?" asked Emily surprised by his quick response. "I'd hate to have you cancel your plans."

"I have none," he replied honestly. "I was just going to hang out, watch a movie, and take it easy."

"You're the best, thank you. I'll see you soon, bye," she said hanging up.

"He's coming, isn't he?"

"Yep, be here in an hour."

"Yay!" she said as she danced around the living room with her mom.

"I need to get ready," said Emily as she started for the stairs, "listen for the door."

An hour later the doorbell rang, and Ava ran to open it. "Michael!" she screamed excitedly.

"Hi, Ava," he said walking in.

"What's in the bags?" she asked curiously.

"Nothing important," he said casually.

"Michael!" she replied not believing him. "Come on, what's inside?"

"Fun," he said with a goofy voice and look that made her laugh. "Are you ready for an enjoyable night?"

"I am."

"Good, because I have lots for us to do."

"You do," she said eagerly, "like what?"

"Was that Michael?" asked Emily as she walked into the room. She was wearing a short, fitted black dress with black high heels, and her hair was curled around her shoulders.

"Wow, Emily you look stunning!" said Michael.

"Thank you," she said as she spun around.

"You look like a model, Mom," added Ava.

"What do you think, red lipstick?" she asked looking at Michael.

"Definitely red," he replied and realized he was staring. "Right, Ava?"

"Yep, definitely, it's a Christmas color."

"Okay, I'll be back in minute," she said leaving the room.

When she returned the two of them were going through one of the bags Michael had brought. "Mom, Michael went to the dollar store and bought us things to make decorations and cards with. He has colored paper, glitter glue, little bells, stickers, beads, popsicle sticks, ribbons, and a whole bunch of other stuff," she said before grabbing the next bag. "What's in here?" she asked looking through it. "Christmas movies! Candies!"

"Hope you don't mind her having candies?" asked Michael.

"Are you kidding? Knock yourselves out. I'm actually kind of jealous, I wish I could stay," she said as the doorbell rang, and she opened it.

"Everyone is going to be envious of me, and you tonight," said Brad walking through the doorway. "We both look awesome!"

"Hi, Brad," said Ava.

"Hi, Munchkin," replied Brad which was met with a disapproving face.

"Brad, this is my friend Michael, Michael my friend Brad."

"Hello," said Michael standing and shaking his hand. He hadn't realized she was going on a date with the guy who had hugged and kissed her at the bar.

"Michael is an angel, he is watching Ava tonight, and it was very last minute" explained Emily. "The babysitter called me saying she was sick, I thought I may have to cancel on you."

"Well lucky for me you're here to help us out, eh sport," said Brad, condescendingly tapping Michael on the shoulder.

"Yes, I guess you are," he replied. "I'm sure Emily deserves a night off work to enjoy herself."

Emily had suddenly realized she had put Michael in a very awkward position and felt bad. She should have told him over the phone who had invited her before asking him to babysit, and what made matters worse, was the way Brad was acting.

"We should get going," said Brad opening the front door. "Wine, dinner, and dancing await us."

"Brad, let me get my coat and say goodbye. I'll meet you at the car."

"Good night all," he said with an exaggerated wave to Ava and Michael, and then turned to Emily, "your Mercedes awaits you, when you're ready," then left.

Emily was a little upset, so after she got her coat, she asked Michael to join her in the kitchen for a minute. "I'm sorry, I should have told you who had invited me before asking you, I have put you in such an awkward position."

"Well, yes and no," he replied. "Yes, it would have been nice to have been informed prior, at least I would have known what to expect; and no, because even if you had have told me, I still would have come over and helped you out."

"Thank you so much," she said sadly. "I'm so sorry."

"It's all right, you go and have a great time. Ava and I have decorations to make, movies to watch, candies to eat, and as soon as you leave, pizza to order," he explained, trying to make her feel better. "We'll be fine."

"Thanks again," she replied hugging him affectionately.

"You should go, you don't want to be late," Michael said as they separated, "your Mercedes awaits you."

Emily giggled and hit him playfully with her small purse. "Okay, enough, I'll be back at twelve, and you have my number if you need me."

"I do," he replied following her into the living room.

"Ava, I know if I tell you to go to bed early you won't, and I know Michael won't make you go either. So, just be a good girl for him and have fun, honey."

Ava jumped up, gave her mom a kiss, and said goodbye as she locked the door behind her. Ava looked at Michael. "I don't like it when Brad calls me Munchkin, I'm almost nine years old."

"Practically, a young lady," suggested Michael.

"Yes, I am. In fact, I am, 'Young Lady Ava of Aurora," she said dramatically, then laughed as she jumped over the couch next to him.

"Do you think we should order some royal pizza my young lady?" asked Michael with an English accent.

"Definitely!"

Emily could hear Ava laughing as she walked to the car and smiled. After she jumped in, Brad started to drive and he waited a while making small talk, before asking. "How did you meet Michael?"

"He came into the bar a few days ago before I was closing, it was dead, so we started talking."

"Is he from Aurora?" he asked, wondering if he was a local.

"He said he grew up here, moved back a year ago, and his parents still live here."

"What does he do?" asked Brad pondering what kind of coin he made.

"He's a writer."

"That's interesting, for a blog, newspaper, magazine?"

"No, novels…The night I first met him he had just finished his first manuscript and is sending it off to publishers soon," she replied, deciding not to tell him the rest.

"Unpublished," said Brad smugly, "a penniless writer."

"I don't know if he is penniless," she replied sharply, "I never asked him about his finances, we were too busy talking and having fun."

Brad took offence to the having fun part but realized he had gone too far. Besides, he had nothing to worry about, she was with him. "Sorry Emily, I didn't mean it like that," he lied. "I meant it like you see in the movies, you know a penniless writer trying to publish their first big novel."

Emily looked out the window, she wasn't sure if his apology was genuine or not, she was leaning more to the side of not.

Chapter 6

Around twelve, Michael noticed Brad's car pull into the driveway and listened to it idling for several minutes, before hearing the car door open and close. This was then followed by footsteps, the front door opening, and Emily walking in.

"How did your night go?" she asked interestedly.

"We had a lot of fun. She's a great girl and no trouble whatsoever. She's asleep under the blankets on the couch," replied Michael pointing to her. "She lasted till eleven."

Emily walked over and looked at her daughter's sleeping face then turned to Michael. "Can you carry her up to her bedroom for me?"

Michael picked Ava up, followed Emily up the stairs and placed her on the sheets that Emily had overturned, and then left while Emily tucked her in. When Emily came downstairs Michael was waiting by the front door with his coat on.

"Do you have to go? Can you stay for a beer? Well, unless you want to get going?" she asked awkwardly. "Of course, you want to get going, what am I thinking. I'm sure you must have things to do tomorrow."

"Well, no, nothing. I can stay," he replied. "Do you want me to stay?"

"Yeah, I would like the company…I mean, yes, I would like you to stay and have a beer with me …because I could do with a beer or two after tonight," she said laughing nervously.

"Okay," he replied with a kind smile.

"Would you mind grabbing a couple from the fridge while I get changed?"

"Sure," he said taking off his coat and going into the kitchen.

Emily came back and stuck her head around the corner. "You don't mind if I throw on my pajamas?"

"No, of course not, get comfortable."

A few minutes later she returned wearing flannel pajama pants, a T-shirt, no makeup, and her hair in a ponytail; Michael thought she looked beautiful.

"Did you make decorations?" she asked.

"Yeah, we made quite a few, plus cards."

"Where are they?" she asked looking around.

"Ava knew she would fall asleep before you came home, so she hid them, she wants to show you them tomorrow morning."

"Oh, okay," she said snickering at her daughter's antics then sipping her beer. "What else did you two get up to?"

"We watched a movie, ate lots of junk food, ordered pizza," he said leaning over and opening the box, "there's some left."

"There is? I'm starving," said Emily reaching in and pulling out a big slice.

Michael watched her devour the pizza and couldn't resist. "What, no food at the party?" he asked in a comical voice.

Emily with her mouth full, quickly covered it, laughed, then swallowed. "They had hot hors d'oeuvres, appetizers, cheese plates, fruit plates, and little sandwiches with the crusts cut off. It was very chic, charming, and probably very expensive; but you really couldn't load up your plate and then wolf it all down."

"Speaking of a wolf, after seeing you rip that pizza apart," said Michael, "I think you saved them from something that I will never be able to forget for as long as I live."

"Oh please," she said chuckling, "so now you're traumatized for life?"

"I believe I am," he said sadly.

"That being the case, I may as well have a second slice," she said reaching into the box, giving him a smile, and continuing with her story. "They also had these fancy wines and champagnes but not one beer in sight." She lifted up her pizza and beer, saying, "cold pizza, cold beer, and

I'm all yours." Emily quickly realized what she said. "Well, you know what I mean."

"I do," he said, "you're a cheap date."

"Hey, you," she replied trying to sound upset before breaking out into a giggle. "I really shouldn't put it all down. It was very elegant, the people were very cordial, and they went out of their way to make me feel welcome."

"Sounds like you had wine, and dinner to some extent, as your date had promised," he jested making her laugh. "Did you dance, too?" he asked, which made her laugh louder.

"Not at all, they had a pianist followed by a string quartet, it was very refined. It was like something you would hear at a luxurious wedding reception dinner," she said finishing her last bite of pizza. "So, it was a little disappointing." Emily noticed Michael grinning to himself. "What?"

"You just reminded me of a wedding reception that was the total opposite to your Christmas party," he replied.

"Tell me about it," she said getting comfortable.

Michael lay back on the couch and faced her. "I went to this wedding once at a beautiful five-star hotel in the city where they had a hundred and twenty guests.

"A five-star hotel, the meal must have been fantastic?" she asked enthusiastically.

Michael started laughing.

Emily wasn't sure why. "What's so funny?"

Michael continued to chuckle.

"Tell me!" she pleaded as she moved closer to him.

It took him a while to stop. "For the appetizers, they brought a platter to every table, you know the kind guys get when they're watching NFL games on a Sunday afternoon at the bar. It was full of wings, mozzarella sticks, jalapeno poppers, fried mushrooms, that kind of stuff, as well as fresh cut veggies with dip."

"You're making this up?" she asked, unsure.

"No, I swear," he said and continued. "Dinner was a banquet burger or hot dog, with a choice of fries, salad, or soup."

"You're pulling my leg?"

"I'm not," he said laughing.

Emily started to laugh with him.

"For dessert, they gave everyone a bowl of vanilla ice cream, and in the middle of the table they placed an assortment of toppings and whipped cream." Michael started to chuckle again.

"To make your own sundaes! No way?"

Michael nodded his head continuing to laugh as she joined in again.

"But they must have had wine?" she asked thinking they couldn't get away with that.

"Nope, the waiters brought pitchers of beer."

"You're kidding! Pitchers of beer, now that's my kind of wedding!" she declared. "I'm guessing they must have had a DJ?"

"Nope," replied Michael. "The groom's brother was in a band, so they had him as their entertainment for the night. They played all the hits, even some oldies, but their songs all had this really heavy rock edge to them. I remember watching all these people, you know young kids all the way up to eighty-year old's, dancing to this music; it was a lot of fun."

"Now that sounds like a good time!" she said not realizing she was practically shoulder to shoulder with him. Emily thought for a minute. "What about a wedding cake? They must have had a wedding cake?"

Michael stopped laughing and got serious, "Yeah, unfortunately they did have a wedding cake."

"Oh, so they did have something traditional?" she asked thinking it's difficult to avoid not having that but then noticed Michael was trying not to laugh. "Okay, what was it made of?"

"Jell-O!"

"Jell-O?" she asked.

"And booze."

"Jell-O and booze! Don't tell me they cut it into squares and gave everyone Jell-O shots?" she asked sitting up.

"That did," replied Michael nodding his head, leaning back on the couch, and laughing. Emily leaned back and joined him.

"You made that up?" she asked playfully.

"No, it's a true story," he said looking at her somewhat dubious look. "I'll show you pictures one day, if you like?"

"No, I believe you," she replied, which she did. "Although maybe one day you can show me them to me, I think they would be a lot of fun to see."

"I will," replied Michael, "you will love them."

She looked at him for a minute then shyly asked. "What are you doing tomorrow?"

Michael made a motion with his eyes and face as if he was going through all the things he had to do.

"Really!" she said giving him an 'are you kidding me look.' "You have nothing to do, right?"

"Right," he replied looking at her. "I've been so busy on my manuscript that I'm finding I don't know what to do with all this free time I have on my hands now," he confessed.

"Then let me help you," said Emily. "Tomorrow morning, we are going to cut down our Christmas tree, would you like to come with us?"

"I don't want to intrude," said Michael cautiously. "Do you want to ask Ava if it's okay first?"

"Well, you won't be intruding, but if that makes you feel comfortable, I will. I'm pretty sure I know what her answer will be," she said with a smile. "I'll call you if there is an issue, otherwise, we'll pick you up at ten?"

"Okay," he replied happily as he watched her put her beer on the coffee table.

Emily turned to look at him, catching his stare. "What?"

You're beautiful, he thought. "Nothing, I should get going, you know, early start in the morning," he said standing, reaching for his coat, and putting it on.

Emily walked with him to the door. "Thanks again for tonight."

"Honestly, she is no problem, and is a wonderful girl."

"No, not just that," she revealed, "hanging out with me, it was really nice." She leaned over and gave him a hug.

He awkwardly hugged her back. "Goodnight, I'll see you in nine hours."

"I'll see you then, goodnight," she replied, closing the door behind him, and leaning on it. "Nine hours," she whispered with a grin.

Michael walked home, happy, but confused.

Chapter 7

"Do you do this every year?" asked Michael.

"Since Ava has been a little girl, it's a family tradition now," replied Emily, "and it's always the same day as the Santa Claus parade."

"That's a wonderful tradition," he said glancing over his shoulder at the back seat. "Are you ready to pick the perfect tree?"

"I am," she said excitedly. "I'm so glad you came with us."

"Thank you for inviting me," he said looking at her glowing face.

"Is it much further, Mom?"

"It's not far, maybe another ten minutes," confirmed Emily looking into her rearview mirror at Ava then over at Michael. "I'm glad you came, too."

They drove down a country road passing the cars and vans parked on either side before pulling into a vacant spot. Then jumped out of the car and followed the snowy path into the entrance of the tree farm. Off to their left, a family looked on as a machine netted their tree, and a little further to their right was a small historical house where groups of families were mingling outside. And just next to the house, was a bonfire surrounded by wooden benches, which occupied several people drinking hot chocolate. As they walked closer, a horse-drawn wagon pulled in front of the house letting passengers with their trees off and people who needed one, on.

"Wait?" asked Michael as he reached for his cell phone. "Let me get a picture of you two with the background." They stopped and smiled as he took their picture.

"Hold on young man, let me take one of you with your family," said a male voice from behind. Michael turned to face an elderly man approaching with his wife, daughter, husband, and grandchildren. "Well actually we are not—"

"That's very kind of you," interrupted a voice standing next to him. "Come on honey," said Emily pulling him next to Ava.

Ava stood in between her mom and Michael as they waited for the man to figure out how to take the picture. Eventually his daughter intervened, took the picture, and walked over to them.

"My father has a heart of gold, but when it comes to cell phones, he's all thumbs," explained Anna apologetically and handing the phone back. "Is this your first time?"

"No, we've been coming here since Ava was a little girl," replied Emily.

"My parents brought us here when we were children, too, now I bring them, my husband, and our children," she said looking over at them. "It's a lovely family tradition."

"I know what you mean," said Emily as she put her arm around Ava and the other one through Michael's. "We look forward to it every year."

"Can I be honest with you?"

"Please do," said Emily.

"It's lovely seeing a young family also starting these family traditions," she said looking at Emily, Michael, then at Ava. "One day, when you are older, you can bring your mom and dad," she said giving her a friendly smile.

"I will," she replied shyly.

They talked for several more minutes, said goodbye, then walked over to the house and picked out a saw before climbing onto the wagon along with several others. With their legs hanging over the side, the wagon slowly pulled away. The horse took them down a small, winding, road to the back of the farm where it stopped, and they jumped off. From here they followed one of the snow-white trails through the trees, and after twenty minutes of searching, Ava found the perfect one.

"I found it! I found it!" she screamed animatedly.

"Oh, this is beautiful, Ava!" said Emily. "It will look perfect in our living room. What do you think, Michael?"

"I thinks it's the best tree I have ever seen!"

"Yay!" said Ava happily jumping and clapping her hands.

"Ava why don't you stand with your mom in front of the tree so I can take a picture?" asked Michael. After he did, he lay down on the ground and started to cut, it was difficult going at first and the girls couldn't help giggling as he struggled. Hearing them laughing he poked his head from under the tree. "Oh, you think this is funny?" he asked good-naturedly.

"Hilarious," replied Ava still laughing with her mother.

"Oh, and you're recording me as well," he said, noticing Emily was videoing him.

"It's bound to get over a million hits on You Tube tonight," Emily suggested.

"Well, I think…" he started to say, and was gesturing with his free hand, when he accidentally touched the tree's branch resulting in a pile of snow falling onto his face and into his open mouth making him cough.

The girls laughed loudly.

"Make that two million, Mom!"

Making them laugh louder.

Michael laughed with them as he placed his head on the ground. Emily knelt next to him and gently wiped the snow from his face. They looked deeply into each other's eyes; they both knew you can tell a lot about someone by looking into their eyes, and they both saw the same thing.

"You okay, Michael?" asked Ava interrupting their moment and looking over him.

"Yeah, you want to finish cutting it?" he asked.

"No," she replied as she knelt next to him and kissed him on the forehead, "you're doing an amazing job."

Michael finished cutting the tree, then the three of them carried it back to the spot where they were dropped off and took the wagon back. They put the tree by the netting machine, went inside the house, and got hot chocolate with marshmallows. Then came outside, sat next to the bonfire, and sipped their drinks while they watched the flames dance to the sound of the crackling wood. After Ava finished, she left to go help the granddaughters build a snowman.

"I love being here," said Emily, "having all these people around, watching the children play, drinking hot chocolate, and feeling the warmth of the fire. It makes you feel good inside and appreciate what's important in life."

"I can't argue with you there," agreed Michael looking around with her. "It's very special."

Emily was thinking about something. She was a little unsure whether to ask him or not, because she didn't want to put him on the spot, after a minute of debating back and forth she decided she would. "Do you want to come with us to the Santa Claus Parade this evening?"

Michael's immediate response was yes; instead, he hesitated, and went quiet.

Emily noticed it straight away. "I've put you on the spot, I didn't mean to, I'm so sorry," she said feeling embarrassed for asking him and saddened by his hesitation.

Michael glanced over at Ava playing, realizing she was occupied, he felt it was safe to talk. "Where's Brad?" asked Michael bluntly.

Emily was a little taken aback by his directness but understood why he was asking. "He's away on a business trip and won't be back till Monday."

Michael thought about her answer. "To be truthful, I don't think I am too comfortable with him coming back to find out what we've been doing, and…" said Michael, he wasn't too sure how to say what was next on his mind without offending her but he couldn't find any other words, "if it were me, I wouldn't like my girlfriend off doing things with someone else while I was away."

"But it's not like that, you're not just someone else," she said in her defense. Oh, damn, she thought, now she has to tell him. "Brad knows we are friends and he's okay with it."

"He knows we're just friends?" he asked curiously.

"Yes, just friends," she repeated as her heart sank.

"And he's okay with it?"

"Michael, girls have male friends," she replied, avoiding his actual question. Sure, Brad was okay with Michael being her friend but to what degree was another question.

Michael reflected momentarily. True, they were only friends, and some girls do have male friends. Plus, her boyfriend had already met him and he's okay with it. And the friendship borders have been set. Michael glanced over at her pleading face and smiled. How could he resist? "Okay, I'll go."

Her heart rose. "Yay!" she yelled louder than expected, making everyone look, then gave him a hug.

"By the way, friends don't hug," whispered Michael.

"Oh, be quiet! Yes, they do!"

He hugged her back as she smiled over his shoulder.

"You two are so adorable and so in love," said Anna as she walked by.

They let go of one another they talked and watched the fire for a while before being pulled over to take pictures of Ava with her friends and the snowman. After that, they picked up the netted tree, tied it to the top of the car, and drove home. Then carried it into the house, placed it into the waiting tree stand, and once secure, maneuvered it into position in the corner. Satisfied, they stood back and admired their tree.

"Now it's time for another tradition, our post-tree cutting breakfast," stated Emily, "which is bacon, eggs, pancakes, toast, orange juice, and coffee."

The three of them worked busily in the kitchen. Michael cooked the bacon, Emily made the eggs and pancakes, while Ava made the toast, set the table, and poured the juice. Once it was ready, they sat around the kitchen table, ready to eat.

Emily lifted up her glass of juice, Ava and Michael lifted theirs. "Here's to Ava for picking out our perfect tree and to Michael for cutting our perfect tree."

"And to Emily, for this delightful breakfast, and the joy she brings," added Michael, making her blush.

They said cheers, clinked glasses, and talked and laughed as they ate.

Chapter 8

"He lives just around this corner," explained Emily as they turned onto Michael's street, "we're almost there."

"I can't wait to see the parade," she said skipping, "and seeing Santa is going to be so much excitedly."

"Here we are," said Emily, "he said we need to walk down the right side of the house, to the back, and knock on the door."

"Hey, guys, come on in," said Michael, "I'll just be a minute."

"Wow, this is beautiful!" said Emily looking around. "I love the open concept kitchen with an island, dining room, and living room. It looks so spacious and modern!"

"Here let me give you a quick tour," he said. Then leaned over to Ava, who he knew was patiently waiting to get to the parade, and whispered, "trust me it will be very, very quick," and began. "Here is the bathroom with a two-person shower and next to it is the spare bedroom. You've already seen the kitchen, dining room, living room. Follow me to the back, over there is a gas fireplace, around this corner, and through this door is my bedroom."

"I love this place! It's so cozy," complimented Emily, "and your furnishings are beautiful!"

"Thank you."

"Michael," said Ava," my mom said this is called a walkout basement apartment, what's that mean?"

"I'll show, come over here," replied Michael, as they followed him past the dining room table. "Are you ready?"

"Ready," she said curiously.

"Behind these curtains," he said opening them, "is a large patio door that I can slide open," which he did, "and it lets you walk out to the backyard."

"That's so amazing," exclaimed Ava, "and it's so big!"

"Wow, that is one big yard, you can play football on it!" she said glancing at Michael. "The tenants upstairs, they don't have access to it?"

"No, they have their own private decks, which gives me lots of privacy," he explained. "In the daytime, I can pull back the curtains to admire the view, and at night sit outside to watch the stars." He looked down at Ava. "The neighbor's orange and white cat likes to sit right there on that padded patio chair," he said pointing, "especially when it is raining, it keeps her warm and dry. Down in the back, there is a bunny rabbit that I've seen at dawn and dusk chewing on the grass. I've also seen a raccoon and its family, as well as a skunk, digging for grubs late at night."

"That is so cool!" cooed Ava.

As Michael closed the doors and curtains, Ava looked around the house noticing something was missing. "You don't have your decorations up yet?"

"This year I'm going to be putting them up closer to Christmas Eve," he explained.

"We're decorating our tree and living room tonight, after the parade, can you come and help us? Please!"

"Ava, I'm sure Michael has other plans tonight after the parade," said Emily, "and don't forget, he watched you last night."

"Do you have other plans?" asked Ava searchingly.

"Ava!" said her mother disapprovingly.

"I'm sorry Michael," she said softly.

Michael looked at her sad face.

"Ava, why don't we get going to the parade?" suggested Emily.

"Yay, let's go!" cried Ava hurrying off to the door.

"I'm sorry about that, we both seem to put you on the spot."

"It's fine," replied Michael who was delighted Ava had wanted to include him. "It was kind of her to ask me."

"You know you are more than welcome to join us after the parade."

"What happened to not putting me on the spot?" he asked humorously.

"Ah, live with it!" replied Emily.

"Does a friend, help a friend, decorate their tree?" he teased.

"My friend Michael does," replied Emily, then corrected herself. "Well, he can, if he wants?"

"Okay, old buddy, old pal of mine," he said putting his arm around her as they walked to the door, "you've got yourself some decorating help tonight."

Emily was delighted. "Thank you," she said with a pretty smile.

They set up a blanket on the sidewalk by the curb, before sitting on it, and stretching their feet out onto the road. Emily covered them with layers of blankets then they snuggled closely and waited for the parade to start. Slowly the electric floats glided by, lighting up the evening night, and filling the air with their festive music as people clapped and cheered. One by one they passed, and two hours later the final float arrived, it was Santa's. He was standing in his sleigh with his eight reindeer in front of him, on a snow-covered rooftop, waving to the crowd. Ava jumped up from under the covers screaming his name and waving frantically. Santa looked right at her, waved back, and shouted, "Merry Christmas!"

"Did you see that?" she asked excitedly. "He waved at me. Santa waved at me!"

After Santa's float passed by, the parade came to an end, and they folded up the blankets and left. Emily and Michael looked on, as Ava happily skipped and talked about Santa the whole way home. One inside, they took off their jackets and boots, and then Ava took off upstairs.

Chapter 9

"The decorations are in the attic but let me show you around the place first, let's start down here," she said leading him down a set of stairs. "This is the basement, as you can see it's finished, and has a full bathroom. Through this door is the washer, dryer, and behind that door there is a big storage area along with the water heater and furnace." She took him up to the main floor. "You already know the kitchen," she said pointing, "and the living room," as they walked through it. She opened French doors off to the side. "In here is the unfurnished dining room, if we continue through to these doors, we come out by the powder room, stairs, hallway, and kitchen. Up here," said Emily as they climbed the steps, "is a full bathroom, behind this door is a spare bedroom which Ava also uses as a playroom, and this is,...," she said knocking on the door. "Can we come in?"

"Yes, Mom."

"Ava's room…Good, you have your pajamas on and tidied up, well, a little."

"Do you like it?" asked Ava looking at Michael with her arms open wide.

"I think it's the best room in the house," replied Michael looking at her, then her stuffed animals, toys, doll house, and décor. "You have lots of pink and purple."

"They are my two most favorite colors," she said. "Do you like them?"

"I think they are very pretty, just like you," he said, and with his finger touched her on the nose.

She grabbed his finger holding on to it. "Let's go see Mom's room."

Emily opened the door and showed him around. "This is mine. It has a walk-in closet, full bathroom, and a view of the backyard."

"Wow, this is a lovely room!"

"Thank you," she replied as they walked out of her room, followed her down the hallway, and up the stairs. "Behind this door is our attic," she said opening it.

"This is incredible!" exclaimed Michael following them in. "It's carpeted, has windows, and painted walls," he said turning to her. "You could use this as an office, bedroom, or play area. It's really beautiful."

"I know, it truly is, we both love it," she said strolling over to the boxes in the corner. "Here are the decorations."

Ava took a small box and went down the stairs while Emily and Michael started putting aside the larger ones.

"How come you haven't furnished this room, the dining room or basement, and use them?" asked Michael picking one up.

"Well, with there just being the two of us, we don't have the need to use them right now," she explained.

"That makes sense."

"I guess it's quite a big place for just the two of us," continued Emily.

Michael put the box down by the window and looked out, Emily joined him.

"You have a big yard, too,"

"It's a good size, not as big as yours," she snickered, "but good enough."

"If you don't mind me asking, how did you come about this place?"

"Not at all," she said. "A couple of years ago an older cousin of mine, Valerie, lived here on her own. She made good money, met a guy who was loaded, and they fell in love. They were moving to New York City and Valerie knew I was renting a place, so she asked me if I wanted to live here. I knew she owned the house outright and that she would give me an excellent rate. I said I would love to and would take diligent care of it for her." Emily paused and collected her thoughts. "You see in the past, I had fallen on some hard times, and she'd helped here and there with money, and paying my bills. But this time, Valerie said she really wanted to help give me a fresh, new, start, so she did, and gave me this house." Emily's eyes started watering and tears started falling. Michael held her as she cried. "I've never told anyone that before," she said sobbing.

"Don't worry your story is safe with me," said Michael reassuringly and handed her tissues from his pocket.

"I know, I trust you," she said, then suddenly realizing he was handing her something. "You're kidding me, you have tissues," she said drying her eyes with them.

"I brought them in case Ava got a runny nose at the parade, you know, some kids get them in the cold…but they work just as well on tears," he said tenderly.

"You're such a kind man," said Emily with a smile, then thanked him with a kiss on the cheek.

"Mom, Michael, are you coming?" interrupted Ava from the bottom of the stairs.

"I don't want her to know I was crying," she said turning her back to the doorway.

"I understand," whispered Michael to her then turned to the doorway. "We are," he shouted down to Ava, "your mom was just showing me the back yard." He looked at Emily and quietly said, "I'll grab the boxes and go downstairs with Ava, which will give you time to slip into your room. I'll just tell her you are taking off your makeup and putting on your pajamas."

"My mascara is running, isn't it?" she said with a hopeless grin.

"Yeah," he replied with a humorous look of repulsion on his face.

"Get out of here you!" she said playfully pushing him.

Michael grabbed a box, went down the stairs, and followed Ava to the living room. They made a couple more trips to the attic until they were done.

"I'm sorry to keep you guys waiting," said Emily strolling into the living room. As she passed Michael she glanced over and mouthed, "thank you."

Michael admired how beautiful and sexy she was as she crossed in front of him.

"What are you doing honey?" she asked stopping in front of Ava.

"I'm making a special, secret card only for Santa to read on Christmas Eve," she replied covering it from her mother. "Only for Santa, Mom."

"Okay, I won't look," said Emily leaning over, putting on Christmas music, and starting towards the kitchen. "I'm going with Michael to make us something to eat while you finish up."

"I won't be long," replied Ava watching her mom leave with Michael before going back to her card.

"I have finger foods that need to go in the oven for twenty minutes, so I will turn the oven on," she explained, which she did. "I also want to make a cheese plate, fruit plate, and veggies with dip," she said turning to Michael. "There's eggnog in the fridge, ice in the freezer, and cinnamon in that cupboard. The rum is on the counter next to two big glasses," she said pointing, "light on the eggnog heavy on the rum."

"Coming right up," said Michael moving to the fridge, "two Icebergs!"

"What? Icebergs?" she said chuckling.

"Yeah, Icebergs, you see them in the water, but you really don't know what's going to happen till you hit them! Or in our case, drink them!"

"Did you just make that up?" she asked doubtingly.

Michael blushed a little. "Yeah, I did."

"Iceberg," she said, "I like it!"

"Here you go, one Iceberg," he said handing her a glass. "Cheers!"

"Cheers!" she replied, clinking his, and taking a sip. "Oh, this is perfect!"

Michael was just about to say, just like you, but caught himself.

Emily put the food in the oven, washed the fruit and veggies, while Michael made up the cheese plate.

"Another five minutes for the food in the oven then we are good to go," said Emily.

"Do you want me to clear some space on the living room coffee table?" asked Michael.

"My card is done," said Ava walking into the kitchen, grabbing a strawberry, and eating it.

"No, Ava and I will do that, you can make us another one of those Icebergs," she said tapping her empty glass.

As they ate, they decorated the tree, stopping once in a while to talk about an ornament which Ava had made or one that had a special memory. Once decorated, Michael lifted Ava up so she could put the star on top of the tree, then they counted down from ten. When they reached zero Emily turned on the tree lights and they joyfully cheered. Ava then put her secret Santa card under the tree, and they were done. Now it was time for pictures. Michael took ones of Ava and Emily in front of the tree, then Emily took some of Ava and Michael, then it was Ava's turn.

"Ready?" asked Ava.

"We're ready," they both replied standing next to one another.

Ava moved the cell phone away from her face. "You need to put your arms around one another. Work with me people!" she said breaking into a loud laughter. "I always wanted to say that!"

Emily was the first to put her arm around his waist, then he put his around her shoulder. She moved in closer, then he did.

"Got it people! That's a wrap!" she said falling back on the couch and chuckling at her words.

As they removed their arms, Emily and Michael slowly looked at each other. "I think I need another drink," whispered Emily.

"I'll get you one," replied Michael leaving for the kitchen.

Emily realized she was blushing.

When Michael came back in, they finished decorating the living room, turned off the room lights, and sat on the couch admiring their glowing Christmas tree.

"This is just as magical as being at the bonfire today," said Emily.

"I love this mom," said Ava snuggling into her, and within no time was asleep.

Chapter 10

Emily stoked her daughter's hair and turned to Michael. "I wanted to finish off my story from the attic, if that's okay?"

"Yes, if you want to?"

"I do," she replied, "I would really like you to now the whole story." She took a long sip of her drink and began. "Before I moved into this place, the furniture I had was either old or second hand. So, I put aside what was special to me and threw out the rest. At the time, I also had this old car that was on its last leg, and decided I needed a new one. Since I had no mortgage on this place, I went to the bank and took one out against the equity of the house. Not a big one, but enough to get the furniture you see here and my car. I also put a little extra in my account for a rainy day," she said and hesitated momentarily. "I managed to get by on my salary and tips but over the last few months it hasn't been easy. Like I said to you earlier, this house, although beautiful, is big and the utilities can be expensive, especially during wintertime. Plus, I had my living expenses. On top of all that, I now had a mortgage. So, my extra money dwindled quickly." She paused again, took a sip of her drink, and thought as she watched the lights twinkling on the tree. "It's difficult being on my own. If Ava gets sick, I have to take care of her, and miss work. If a babysitter can't make it after school, I have to leave work early. Even when I do take on an additional shift, by the time I pay the babysitter it ends up not being worth my while going in, which means I have to limit my shifts around Ava being at school or when she is visiting my parents for the weekend. So, for the last little while things have been difficult for me, financially. I was thinking about going to the bank to refinance but I don't want to end up being in the same position again several months down the road. I also thought about selling this, and renting something nice like you have, but I really don't want to leave this place; I love it here. I'm not sure what to do?" she said sadly. "Unfortunately, I know I have to decide on something soon."

"I can only imagine how difficult it must be being a single mom," said Michael, "but you've done a wonderful job raising Ava."

"Thank you," she said managing a smile.

"The positive is that you have two options as opposed to none," he added trying to be upbeat.

"That's true," she replied as she continued to stare at the tree.

"If you don't mind me asking, how much are you short?"

"It's not much, you may think it's funny," she said giggling nervously. "By the end of the year, over a couple of thousand, and that takes into account Christmas spending minus the few extra shifts I can take." She looked away from the tree at Michael. "The problem is next month it will be three thousand, the month after thirty-five hundred, and so on. I'll never catch up or get ahead."

Michael thought as he looked at her "I can give you the money?"

"No," she replied assuredly, "I couldn't let you do that but thank you for offering."

"How about I loan you the money? You can pay me back over time."

Emily gave him a tender look. "No, I don't want to borrow from one person to pay another," she explained appreciating his thoughtfulness. "This is something I need to do and figure out on my own, does that make sense?"

"It does," replied Michael as they both looked at the tree deep in thought, then suddenly it came to him. "How about this? If you need someone to watch Ava, ask me, anytime. That will give you the flexibility to take on additional shifts, late shifts, double shifts, and shifts on a school night. I can watch her here, help her with homework, and make her dinner."

"I can't put all that on you." she said looking at him.

"I've already told you I'm taking some time away from my writing and how I've been cooped up for nine months. It would be good for me to get out and do something. I have no set plans, and I also have lots of free time," he said keenly. "But more importantly, me watching Ava is not only going to help you save money but help you make money. Just think about all the extra shifts you can take. Please, let me help you, and come January you can reevaluate your situation."

"Why would you do that for me?" she asked as her eyes filled up.

"That's what friends do," he replied squeezing her hand. "Listen, you don't have to decide now, take some time and think about it."

Emily realized she now had a third option, the best option. She slowly shook her head. "I don't have to think about it," she said lifting his hand, pressing it against her cheek, and kissing it softly. "I'll take you up on that, thank you," she said fighting back her tears.

"Good, when do you need me to start?" he asked eagerly. "And is there anything you need to do first?"

Forgetting about Ava, she was about to jump up. "Let's put her to bed first," she said. "Can you carry her?"

Michael followed Emily, placed Ava in the unturned bed, and waited for her downstairs.

"She's all tucked in," said Emily entering the room. "Can you grab a couple of drinks? I'm going to get my phone."

Michael poured them then sat next to her on the couch.

"First, I'll text my boss to let him know if there are available shifts, or if some do come available, to let me know. Second, text all the staff that if they need someone to cover any of their shifts to contact me."

Michael sipped his drink and watched her.

"That's done!" she said taking her drink from Michael. "Is it best if I just text you the days and times, like a meeting request?"

"That would be perfect, that way I can add them to my calendar."

"Give me a few minutes, there done!" She thought for a moment. "I think that's it…Oh, no, the babysitter. I need to text her and let her know I don't need her for the ones I just sent you…actually, that I don't need her anymore."

"Is she going to be upset?"

"I doubt it, I think she'll be fine, she's a teenager who has a new boyfriend," she said texting her. "That's done!"

"Now, when you get additional shifts just text me like you did, and once I receive it, I will accept it. Then you will get a confirmation reply from me knowing it's been accepted."

"Okay," she said feeling relieved, "thank you so much, you don't know what this means to me." She leaned over, kissed him gently on the cheek, and before he could say it. "Yes, friends kiss friends on the cheek, so deal with it. Especially ones that are helping me out and I'm thanking!"

"You beat me to it," he declared.

"I did," she replied smiling happily at the fact. "So, what are plans for tomorrow afternoon?"

"Nothing, I have a pitiful life," he replied sadly.

"You writers are so melodramatic," she said chuckling.

"Tis true," he replied miserably making her laugh louder. "Why do you ask?"

"Ava is going to a birthday party tomorrow afternoon for a few hours, do you want to do something? Nothing fancy, maybe grab a coffee, and go for a walk."

"Yeah, I would like that."

"How about we meet around one?"

"One it is."

"Good," she said with a cute smile.

They sipped their drinks, talked about their day and night, how pretty the tree looked and its captivating pine scent.

Emily yawned and Michael realized it was getting late. "I should get going," he said standing to leave.

Emily rose with him, gave him a big hug, and put her head on his chest. "Thank you for everything."

"You're welcome," replied Michael, she felt warm and soft. "Thank you for including me in your special day."

"It was a lot of fun having you with us," she said pulling away and walking with him to the door. "I'll see you tomorrow."

"Tomorrow," he reconfirmed. "Goodnight."

"Goodnight," she replied closing the door behind him and turning with a big smile. Her phone beeped, she ran to read it, maybe it was an available shift. Instead, it was a text from Brad: "Sorry I haven't been able to text you sooner. Wining and dining clients. Just arrived back at my hotel room. How was your day and night?"

Chapter 11

"Here we are, Aurora Trails."

"I can't believe it, I haven't walked these in ages, I used to come all the time when Ava was younger," Emily confessed looking around. "Snow-covered trees, the sun is shining; it's so beautiful and so breathtaking."

"It is," agreed Michael. "I love walking through here. These trails and I have gotten to know one another over these past several months."

"They have?" she asked inquisitively.

"When I needed to get out of the apartment to take a break from writing, this is one of the places I would come to. I found it relaxing and inspirational."

"I can understand that it's so peaceful," said Emily and remembered something. "Oh, speaking of writing. I read after you left last night and I'm almost halfway through your manuscript. The characters are wonderful, the setting is beautiful, the storyline and subplots are attention-grabbing and flow seamlessly; I love it so much! It's been difficult for me to put it down. I even read some this morning and was almost late meeting you," she said with a laugh.

"Thank you," he replied, "I'm glad you're enjoying it."

"I have been editing along the way: grammatical errors, content recommendations," she said looking over at him sternly, then smiled, "overall very well-written."

"I can't wait to review your suggestions," said Michael wanting to see them.

"I should be finished on Thursday," she confirmed. "I have to confess; it's been so much fun editing. I truly love it. I'd forgotten how much I enjoyed doing it," she said sipping her coffee. "So, what's the plan once you update all my recommendations?"

"Update all your recommendations?" he asked impishly.

"Yep, I'm pretty confident you will."

"I'm sure I will," he replied giving her a smile, "and to answer your question. I have a friend of the family who's the chief editor at the local paper and he has friends that are publishers. So, he is going to call in a few favors for me so I can send it directly to them."

"That's great, it's always good to have contacts," said Emily, "especially friends of the family."

"Well, he is a friend of the family now, but he wasn't always."

"He wasn't?" asked Emily, confused.

"Let me explain," said Michael chuckling at her expression. "When I was a teenager, a few houses down from where I lived, there was an elderly woman who lived on her own, Mrs. Johnson. At the beginning of summer my dad asked me one day to go cut her lawn. I went, knocked on her door, introduced myself, and told her I was there to cut the lawn. She said okay and told me to come see her when I had finished. After I was done, I knocked on her door again and she invited me. She gave me a glass of lemonade, a sandwich, and homemade cookies. Then she started talking to me about her husband who was in the war, how they met, their children, and grandchildren, and showed me their pictures on her mantle. When it was time for me to go, she handed me money, which I politely refused. My dad never had to ask me again. Every couple of weeks, I would drop by to cut her lawn, go in for my lunch and have a chat. And when winter came, I would shovel her driveway and sidewalk, and do the same thing."

"She was looking for company?"

"Yes," replied Michael taking a drink of his coffee.

"That's so sweet of you," cooed Emily.

"One time she asked me what I wanted to do when I was older. I told her I liked reading and loved to write, and after taking English in college, I want to be a writer of novels. She then explained to me how one of her grandchildren went to military school, then college, and became a journalist. And when he was in his twenties, thirties, and forties, had done lots of pieces covering wars, major events and was very well-known, but had since retired. At that time, I never thought much about it. A couple of years later she became quite ill, had to go live in a nursing home, and eventually passed away."

"Oh, that's sad."

"It was," said Michael thinking of her fondly. "Shortly after her death there was a knock at the door, my father answered, and it was a middle-aged man looking for me. My dad invited him in and called me down. The man introduced himself as Bob Johnson, the grandson of Mrs. Johnson. He said he was the executor of her estate, had just inherited his grandmother's house, and was moving in over the next few weeks. Bob continued to tell us that his grandmother talked about me all the time to him and his family, that she was very fond of me, and about how his mother would go on and on about all the conversations she had with me, how happy it made her, and how she looked forward to seeing me. Then suddenly, Bob stands up military-like saying, and I quote, 'before I continue, I want to thank you, young man, it's an honor and a privilege to finally meet you, and shake your hand,' which he did then we sat down. He mentioned again how he was executor to her estate, and in her will she had mentioned me, Mickey."

"Wait? What? Mickey?" interrupted Emily giggling.

"Okay, okay, when she was younger, she used to watch the black and white Mickey Mouse cartoons. She told me in every Mickey Mouse cartoon she remembers, Mickey was always smiling and happy, just like me. Since my name was Michael, she called me Mickey."

"Oh, that is adorable, Mickey," said Emily, playfully squeezing his cheek. "Actually, I like that nickname too…please, continue."

"Bob said when she said the name Mickey, he knew straight away she had meant me, and this was the reason for him being here. Apparently, she had asked Bob to give me something."

"What? What?" asked Emily impatiently.

"It was a picture she had shown me many times of her, her husband, her children, and her grandchildren at Walt Disney World, and right between her and her husband, was Mickey Mouse. She said being there with all her family, was her favorite trip, and that day with them all getting their picture with Mickey Mouse, was her favorite memory."

"That is so cute, so she gave it to you?"

"She did," said Michael, "but there's more."

"I think I'm going to cry," said Emily. "Tell me, what happened next?"

"The picture was originally in a Walt Disney frame that she had bought during their stay, only Bob hands me the picture and frame separately. I give Bob this puzzled look, and he tells me his grandmother wrote something on the back."

"Oh no, what did she write," said Emily putting her arm through his. "I am going to cry."

"She wrote, 'This is a picture of me, my family, and my second favorite Mickey, Thank You, God Bless, Love Bea.'"

Emily squeezed his arm. "That is so beautiful, she really loved you."

"Yeah, she was a wonderful lady," said Michael reflecting momentarily before glancing over at Emily, "but that's not all."

"Tell me, tell me!" she begged.

"After Bob gave me the picture, he said his grandmother had told him about how I wanted to go to college to study English. He informs me she had set up a yearly grant in her name at the local high school, and it was to be awarded to a graduating student with exemplary marks in English, and who was going to major in English or Journalism at college. The grant would pay for their first-year tuition and was called the Beatrice Johnson English Award. Each year, Bob was to decide the recipient of that award, with the exception of the first recipient. Beatrice wanted to choose that herself, and she chose—"

"You?" asked Emily excitedly. "She gave the grant to you!"

"Well, yes and no."

"Yes and no?"

"Well, yes, she chose me; but no, I didn't get a grant for the first year. For me, she had made an exception, and paid my tuition, books, and expenses for every year I went to college."

"That is incredible!" said Emily overwhelmed. "That was so kind of her."

"To be honest with you, if I hadn't received that award, I'm not sure if my parents would have been able to afford it."

"That makes it all the more special," she added. "Is there more?"

"There is," he replied, "and you will really like this."

"Tell me, tell me, tell me!" she said quickly.

"Bob shakes my hand, tells my dad he should be very proud of me, and leaves. A few weeks later Bob Johnson and his family move in, and the famous Robert Johnson and his wife, and my parents, become exceptionally good friends." Michael waited for it to sink in. He could see her mind turning, and by her facial expression, he knew she was playing back his story in her head.

"Wait! Wait! Hold on! When you say, Robert Johnson, do you mean Robert Johnson, the famous reporter, correspondent, editor?"

"The one and only."

"I can't believe it!" she said shocked.

"When I met him, I didn't know who he was at the time. To me he was a retired journalist, who was now an editor, and used to help me with my papers. Until one day my dad told me who he really was."

"You're telling me Robert Johnson proofread your papers and gave you feedback," she said in awe. "He's what every journalist or editor aspires to be." Emily stopped and thought momentarily. "Wait a second, Robert Johnson is Bob Johnson, the chief editor at the local paper you are talking about."

"One and the same."

"That is so amazing!" she said as the pieces of his story fell into place, then gave him a puzzled look. "Why didn't you get him to edit your manuscript?"

"We did talk about it, but we agreed his background is more journalism not novels, and I would think about it. The other day I told him…" said Michael hesitating.

"Told him, what?" she asked curiously.

"I told him I had found my editor."

"Me! You picked me over Robert Johnson! I can't believe it, are you crazy?"

"No, not at all, I think I made the right choice," replied Michael laughing at her reaction.

"What did Bob think?" Emily queried, unsure if she wanted to know the answer.

"I explained to him who you were and your background. He told me back in his younger days he was driven by passion and enthusiasm, and I needed someone more like that, someone like you."

A big smile came over Emily's face. "Wow, Robert Johnson said someone like me! Well, I'm not going to let you or Bob down," she said determined.

"I know you won't," replied Michael confidently.

Chapter 12

As they continued their stroll, he gave her a while to take everything in before he asked his next question. "Do you like your job?"

"I like the people I work with, the customers. It's close to home and Ava's school."

Michael looked at her skeptically.

"Oh, that's not what you asked," she said, knowing she had avoided answering his question. "No, not really, in fact I despise it."

"Despise it?"

"Maybe that's a harsh word," said Emily chuckling. "I only say that because I feel I'm capable of doing so much more with my life," she explained, giving him a half smile, and holding his arm tightly.

"What ever happened to journalism? Did you get your degree?"

She realized she hadn't told him about college. "Remember I said I was editing for the college paper?"

"I do," replied Michael.

"Well, there was a guy who helped out at the newspaper writing campus stories. At the time, he was a year older and in his final year. So, I edited his stories from time to time. We kind of had the same interests and started dating. To cut a long story short, that's the journalist part of me by the way," she said glancing at him nervously, "I got pregnant." Emily paused, looked down at the ground, and gathered her thoughts. "He told me it was my fault and that he didn't want to be tied down with a child or get married. The first part of what he said I thought was unfair and cruel, he had played a role too and it was his child, but deep down I knew he was right about getting married. It was more of a fling between the two of us and we were just having fun. We hadn't planned on being together after college, getting married, having children; none of that. I knew back then if we would have stayed together and tried to make it work, we would have been unhappy, and it wouldn't have lasted very long. But most importantly, we weren't in love."

"I understand," said Michael sympathetically. "What happened to him?"

"A couple of months later, he graduated, and took off to Europe never to be heard from again. Although later, through a secondhand source—"

"Did you just say secondhand source?" he asked lightheartedly.

"I did, journalist in me, again," she said with a giggle. "My source had heard he married a Spanish girl, and a year later on the news, I heard he was fatally shot in crossfire while reporting."

"I'm sorry to hear that," he said sincerely.

"Thank you," said Emily squeezing his arm. "To be honest with you, I had no deep-rooted feelings for him, we had been apart for a number of years. I only felt sad because I knew him once and we had Ava."

"Does Ava know?"

"I only told her the part about how he died, nothing more."

"That makes sense," said Michael stopping and looking at her. "What did you do after he left you?"

"Me, I quit college one year short of my degree, moved in with my parents and had Ava. I got a job at the bar, and we lived with them for several years. When my parents retired, they moved up north, and wanted us to come with them but Ava and I didn't want to go; we love it here. Instead, I rented a place, continued working at the bar then moved into the place I currently own…you know the rest from there."

They started to walk again and were silent for a while; she wondered what he was thinking, until he spoke.

"Do you ever think about getting back into editing?"

"If I could, I would love to do that," she replied without hesitation, "the reality is I need money which means I need my job."

"Let me ask it another way," said Michael. "If you could do your dream job, what would it be?"

She grinned at him. "You're a persistent little…friend."

"Persistency, kissing cheeks, hugging…apparently that's what friends do," he said teasingly.

"Apparently so," she said with a laugh.

"And yes, I'm still waiting for your answer."

"Just to get you off my back," she said pretending to be annoyed. "I have really enjoyed reading and editing your manuscript. It's been a lot of fun, and I look forward to it every day. The first night we met, remember when you said to me, 'it's work, but it's fun work,' now I know what you mean by that."

"Then why don't you do it?"

"It's not that simple. I just can't quit my job."

"What about doing it part time?" he suggested. "Maybe not now, but after you get caught up financially, perhaps in the new year. I can help you get authors who will actually pay you to get their work edited, even talk to Bob, and see if he needs any help."

"You would do that for me?"

"Of course!" he replied determinedly.

"I don't know," she said glancing at him anxiously. "Do you think I should? Do you think I can?"

"I know you should, and you can, but more importantly, you have to believe you can and in yourself."

"Do you believe in me?"

"I do, one hundred percent."

Emily stopped, turned toward him, and hugged him tightly. "Thank you, that means so much to me."

Michael held her. "There's no rush to decide, you have lots of time to think about it," he said. "Just promise me, at the very least, you will consider it?"

"I promise you, I will," replied Emily, who suddenly realized she now had a fourth option.

They continued their walk and talked about general things like the trails, the trees, and the birds. On the way home, they shared their childhood Christmas stories, and when they arrived at the corner of their streets they stopped and faced one another.

"I had a lovely time today," said Emily grinning. "I like talking with you."

"I like it too," he replied, smiling back. "It's like I've known you my whole life."

"I was just thinking the exact same thing!" she replied playfully tapping his arm before reaching over and hugging him for a while. "I'll be in touch."

"Okay," he replied as he let go and watched her leave.

Emily walked happily down the street, turned around, smiled, and waved. Michael waved back.

Chapter 13

When Emily arrived at her driveway her phone rang. "Hello," she said, then listened. "So, you want Ava to stay a little longer and you'll drop her off at eight?" she reconfirmed, then listened again. "That's fine, I will see you then, bye" she replied and hung up.

"Do you want to get something to eat?"

She was startled by the voice behind her. "Brad! I thought you weren't back till tomorrow?"

"Things wrapped up early. I thought I would come back and surprise you."

"Well, you did!" said Emily caught off guard.

"Ava won't be back till eight?"

"Ah, yeah," she replied, realizing he had overheard her phone conversation.

"Let's go get Italian, there is a delightful little restaurant on Main Street, which has the best linguine in town."

"All right, but I should go changed first," she suggested, starting for her front door.

"No, no need, it's Sunday and it's casual."

Inside the restaurant, they were seated at a table next to a large window that had festive red and green lights around it, and a picturesque view of Main Street. In the background low orchestral Christmas music played, as Brad ordered wine and appetizers for them to share.

"How did your meeting go?" asked Emily, hoping she would spend the majority of their time together listening to him.

"Excellent, we had the deal signed by Saturday evening, which is why I was able to come back today," he replied. Last night he had received a short reply text from her saying everything was good, he was anxious to know the details of what she did. "How was your weekend? Did you get your Christmas tree?"

"We did," she replied putting on a smile. "Michael came with us too."

"I thought you two did it on your own every year?" he said with a surprised look. "Don't you pick out the tree then have one of the farmers cut it down for you?"

"We usually do, but with him helping me out last minute on Friday night, I thought it would be a nice way of thanking him by asking to join us."

"That's thoughtful of you," said Brad, not sure if he believed her or not. "Did you make it to the parade?"

"Yeah, it was lots of fun. Ava was so happy, Santa Claus waved to her."

Brad ignored what she said. "Was Michael there too?"

Emily realized he wasn't interested in the parade. "Uh-huh," she replied understanding where this was going.

"Next you will be telling me he helped you decorate the tree," he half joked.

"Actually, yes, he did!" she snapped back getting upset with his interrogation.

Brad sat back in his chair incredulously. "I don't believe this."

"Well, you should because I'm not going to lie to you," she said in her defense. "And just for the record, at the tree farm he asked me about you and if you would be upset, and I told him what I had told you, that Michael and I are just friends."

"You did?"

"Yes, I did," she said. "He's a wonderful guy and I like his company, but that's all."

Brad relaxed a little. "I'm sorry," he said believing her.

"He has also offered to help me out with Ava, too."

"How?"

"I'm a little behind on my bills so I need to pick up some extra shifts and do some closes. He said if I needed someone to watch Ava he would."

"You don't need to do that, I'll give you the money, how much do you need? This way you wouldn't have to leave her at all," said Brad genuinely. "Give me a number."

"I know you would, thank you, but this is something I need to fix on my own," said Emily appreciating his offer. "You understand that, right?"

"No, not really," replied Brad, "I'm giving you a quick and easy solution." By her expression he realized he had said the wrong thing and quickly tried to fix it. "But if that is what you need to do, then you should do it."

"Thank you," she replied, although she felt he was just saying that to appease her. "I was also thinking, now this is just a thought and not definite, that I may do editing part time in the new year."

"Editing? You mean like articles, newspapers?" he said with an uncertain look.

"Yes, although preferably novels, novellas, and short stories," she explained. "You remember when I told you I did editing for the college newspaper when I was studying for my degree?"

"I do recall you saying that," he replied, which he didn't, "Did you graduate?"

"No, but—"

"Wouldn't someone ask you what your credentials are before you edited their stories for them?"

"Not necessarily," she said, "but they would ask me whom I have edited before?"

"And," he replied knowing he had the upper hand, "what would you say?"

Emily went quiet.

Brad gave her a long look then it came to him. "Did you want to graduate?"

"I always wished I had; it was one of my regrets."

"If you move to the city, in September, you could enroll at the college full time and get your degree. There's an excellent one not too far from where I'm looking to move."

"That sounds interesting," she said leaning forward.

"After you graduate, then you can start your editing, with a degree hanging behind you on your office wall."

"Hmm," she said, "with a degree on my office wall."

He gave her ample time to let it sink in and patiently watched her thinking as he sipped his wine before snapping her back to reality. "Are you ready to order your entrée?"

"What?" she asked. "Oh yes, entrée."

After their meal, Brad dropped Emily off at home. Inside, she made Ava's lunch then sat on the couch deep in thought as she waited for her to be dropped off.

Chapter 14

"How was your Christmas party?" asked Sue as they put up the holiday decorations around the bar.

"The people were friendly and made me feel welcome. All the women wore beautiful dresses, the food was divine, the champagne was expensive, and a pianist followed by a string quartet played Christmas music. It was very charming and pleasant."

Sue stopped what she was doing and gave her a look.

"Okay, okay, the people were somewhat agreeable, the dresses were too flashy, and the food, booze, and music were lame."

"That's better," replied Sue going back to hanging her final decoration.

"When I came home Michael was there and—"

"Say that again?" asked Sue moving towards Emily, her interest piqued.

"My babysitter called and said she was sick. So, he helped me out."

"Continue," she said as she sat down.

"I went upstairs and changed into my pajamas. We had a few cold beers, and I had a couple of slices of pizza. I told him about my lame party, he then told me about a wedding he went to…Oh, listen to this," she said and told her about it.

"A Jell-O wedding cake! That they cut up and served as Jell-O shots!" repeated Sue. "That's my kind of wedding!"

"I know, me too," replied Emily with a grin. "He has all these fascinating stories, and he makes me laugh. We had such a fun time. So…" said Emily stalling.

"So, what?" asked Sue picking up on it.

"I asked him to come with us to the tree farm," said Emily slowly.

Sue almost fell off her chair.

Emily pulled alongside her and turned on her phone. "Look at this picture, this woman thought we were a family, so she took one of the three of us." She went through every picture in detail and ended with the tree cutting video. "After that, we placed the tree in the stand, and made breakfast together. Then he came to the Santa Claus parade with us, and after, helped us decorate the Christmas tree and the living room."

Sue had an odd look on her face.

"What?"

"Which guy are you dating?"

"It's not like that," replied Emily assuredly. "Michael and I talked about it at the tree farm, we're friends, that's it."

"I guess there's no harm in having a male friend," said Sue somewhat unconvinced about whether they were just friends or more.

"That's what I said," she replied with a cheerful smile. "On Sunday afternoon we met, went for a long walk, and talked." Emily then divulged their conversations.

"He wants you to consider editing in the new year?"

"I told you I was editing his manuscript."

"I know, I remember," replied Sue, which she did.

"Well, I really enjoy doing it, it's been a lot of fun," expressed Emily, "and it makes me happy."

"Let me ask you something, does Brad know about all this?"

"Yeah, I told him last night at dinner."

"Dinner!" exclaimed Sue.

"When I left Michael and arrived home, Brad was there. Ava wasn't being dropped off till eight, so he took me to the Italian restaurant down the road; by the way, the food was excellent."

"And Brad?"

"He was okay."

"And he was okay with your friend Michael?"

"I reiterated to Brad, Michael and I, are only friends."

"Okay," replied Sue with a bewildered look.

Then Emily told Sue about Brad suggesting she go back to college to get her degree.

"College? Is that something you want to do? What about editing in the new year?"

"I know," said Emily, "I'm a little confused about that."

"To be honest with you I'm a little confused about all of it!" replied Sue as she walked to the entrance door. "One thing is for sure, your life has been a lot more interesting and exciting since Michael walked through this," she said unlocking it.

Emily couldn't argue with Sue about that, but that wasn't all Michael had brought.

Chapter 15

"I'm sorry I'm so late, we were swamped at dinner time," said Emily closing the front door behind her. "I've never seen it so busy!"

"Don't worry about, I received your text."

"How is she?"

"She went to bed a few hours ago. I let her stay up till eight thirty to watch the end of a Christmas movie, I hope that's okay?"

"It's fine," she said hanging up her coat. "What have you been up to?"

"Just relaxing, sitting looking at Christmas tree, and watching the lights."

"That's exactly what I want to do," said Emil putting on Christmas music. "I'm going to go get changed, are you going to stick around for a while?"

"If you want me to?"

"Of course, I do."

"Would you like a tea?" he offered.

"I would love one, milk and one sugar, please," she replied as she went up the stairs and made a sigh of relief at the thought of being able to relax with a hot cup of tea after a twelve-hour shift. When she came down Michael was in the kitchen. "Did you find everything okay?"

"I did, mostly trial and error. I had to look through a couple of cupboards, but I eventually got there," he replied handing her a cup of tea.

Emily followed Michael into the living room. She let him sit down first, then sat close to him before turning around and placing her head on the armrest and her feet on his lap.

"Long day?"

"Long and busy. I'm so glad to be home," she answered sipping her tea. "Mm, this is good." She looked at him for a while, wanting to ask him his thoughts on something but wasn't sure how to approach him on the subject, and decided it was best to start from the beginning. "When I left you yesterday afternoon Brad showed up here, he had come home a day early because his deal went through quicker than expected, so he took me out for dinner."

"That was thoughtful, where did you go?"

"The Italian restaurant on Main Street, it's very quaint, and the food was excellent."

"Did Ava like it?"

"She wasn't with us," said Emily. "After I left you, I received a call from the birthday girl's mom asking if she could drop her off at eight, I said it was fine."

"Did she have a good time?"

"She had a great time," replied Emily sipping her tea. "During our meal I mentioned to Brad about me doing editing part time in the new year."

"What did he think?"

"He thought I should consider going back to college in September, getting my degree, and then taking on the editing," said Emily, "Brad believes it would be to my advantage to get my diploma first. What do you think?"

"I think it's a decision you need to make."

"Oh," she said and went silent.

"How was he suggesting you get your degree?"

Oh no, she thought, she had put herself in a corner that she knew she couldn't get out of. "Brad received a promotion for VP of Sales, because of that he needs to move to the city, and is planning on buying a condo after Christmas. He asked me if Ava and I would consider moving there with him. Brad doesn't mean tomorrow, it would be after Ava finishes her school year," she explained. "One of the reasons he is asking me now is so he can decide on what sized condo to buy. The bigger picture, I'm guessing, is that he is looking for a commitment from me, so that's why he wants my answer by Christmas Eve. Which brings me to your question, Brad said if I did decide to move, I could enroll in college in September."

Michael gave her a perplexed look.

"What? You're giving me an odd look."

"How long have you known Brad?"

"A couple of months."

"How did you meet him?"

She realized it was time to let him know everything, even though she knew the cost may be high. "Okay," she said and took a deep breath. "A few months ago, I was working at the bar, and he came in with a few friends. He was a little flirty with me but very charming, no, not charming, very confident. Brad would always give me compliments here and there, you know something that a girl would like to hear like, you have pretty eyes, you have a radiant smile, and your hair looks nice did you just get it—"

"I get the picture," interrupted Michael getting a little upset.

"Sorry," she said realizing she had gone a little too far. "Anyway, he was always pleasant and polite. And left generous tips, not only for me, but whoever was working. One night, he asked me out, and I told him I wasn't interested and that I don't date customers, but he was very persistent."

"Not in a friendly way," joked Michael realizing she was opening up to him.

"Oh no, more like a predator," she replied laughing. "A week or so later, Brad tells me he has this friend who owns a high-end restaurant twenty minutes south of here, and he could get me a job there. That I would get better money and bigger tips. I said thanks, but no thanks. He asks me not to be so hasty and to let him take me there for dinner to see for myself. I thought why not and agreed. The place was gorgeous, the food was excellent, and he introduced me to the owner who was extremely nice. On the way home, he asked me if I was interested in working there, and I flat-out said no. He asked me why? I explained to him working mostly evening hours conflicted with Ava and the distance from home and her school was an issue; overall it just wasn't practical for me," said Emily taking a sip of tea. "He was very understanding and said he was sorry to have wasted my time to which I replied he didn't because I had an enjoyable evening. So, he asked me if I would want to do it again some other time, maybe go out with him the following week. So, I—"

"You went out for dinner with him, it wasn't a date because he wanted you to check out this restaurant, then he apologized for wasting your time. Which you felt guilty about, so you agreed on seeing him again?"

"I guess," said Emily still thinking about his question. "You make it sound like there is something wrong with that?" But as she thought more about his comment, she recognized there was merit to what he was suggesting.

"I'm sorry, continue," said Michael feeling bad for putting her on the defensive. Although, he felt he was only pointing out what seemed obvious to him. Then suddenly he realized something else, he now understood how Brad had been promoted to VP of Sales.

"We started dating, maybe ten dates so far, all of them at restaurants including the Christmas party. He's been here once, no twice, for about an hour. Usually to talk about his work, him moving, and asking me if I want to move."

Michael looked at her dubiously. "Do you think that's long enough together to make that kind of commitment?"

"I'm not sure. He's very kind, generous, and someone I feel I can grow with," she replied unconvincingly. "For now, I think he's just looking for a commitment from me to date only him and not others, and then in several months move to the city."

Michael didn't know how to reply; he knew what he should say to her as a friend, and what not to say to her based on his own feelings. Either way, he knew one thing; it was still her decision to make. "Emily, you need to do what's best for you and for Ava."

"I should move."

"No, I didn't say that," said Michael, "you need to think it through and evaluate it all. The best decision, is an informed decision, which means you need to find out as much as you can first."

"I know," she replied hesitantly, "I'm just confused."

"Just take your time, I'm sure you will figure it all out," he said leaning over, putting his hand on her face, and gently caressing her cheek. She responded by arching her head toward it. He slowly moved it away and she wished he hadn't. "Now, to get back to your question about going to college and getting your degree. Is this something you want to do?"

"Like I said to Brad, I always wished I had, and it was one of my regrets," said Emily. "In the past, it was something I considered doing maybe one day, but in saying that, it's never felt like a top priority or a void I needed to fill in my life. In fact, the more I think about it, I actually believe I have learned all I can from college. Doing the newspaper and the hands-on experience is really where I need to focus my attention," she said and thought momentarily. "Although, having a degree would definitely be an asset."

Michael could see the confusion in her eyes and hear it in her voice. "Do you want my take on it?"

"Please, put me out of my misery," she said with a chuckle, "my head is spinning!"

"Okay, how about this," he suggested with a serious look. "If you decide you do want to finish your degree, what Brad is suggesting, is definitely a positive for you moving to the city. For me, the sooner you move the better," he said nonchalantly looking away and making a gesture with his right hand of shooing her away.

"Oh, so you want me to move to the city, trying to get rid of me, huh?" she said standing up and pushing both his hands back as he tried to fight her off. Emily continued to push and knelt on the couch for leverage eventually putting his legs in between her knees; she was now straddling his lap.

"Is this how friends sit?" jested Michael.

"This is how close friends sit," she joked back. They continued play fighting for a while then she stopped suddenly.

Michael noticed something. "Are you okay?"

She put her arms around him and placed her head on his shoulder. "I don't want to lose you," she whispered.

Michael held her for a long time.

She slowly lifted up her head, smiled and softly caressed his messy hair, then moved off his lap and stood up. "I think I need another tea," she said embarrassed about her outburst but more so by his silence. "Do you want one?"

"I'll have another," he replied, "before you go come and sit next to me." After she did, he held her hands, and looked into her eyes. "Whatever you decide, I will always be here for you and Ava. You're never going to lose me, I promise."

Emily managed a smile. "Thank you," she replied, she needed to hear that.

"Come on, I'll help you make the tea."

Chapter 16

"Hello, Brad," she said answering her phone.

"What are you up to tonight?"

"I just got home from work, Tuesday is always a busy day," she explained, "and I'm about to make dinner for Ava and I."

"Did you want me to pick up some takeout?" he asked. "It will save you from cooking."

"No, not tonight, I want to spend some time with Ava. I had to close last night and I'm working tomorrow."

"How about I come over after she goes to bed?" he pressed.

"No, I'm going to continue editing Michael's manuscript, I told him I would have it done by Thursday."

Brad was silent for a moment. "On Friday when you told me you were going to edit his book, I didn't think it was going to cut into our time."

"Hold on a second, we had no plans tonight," said Emily defensively. "This is you asking me last minute because you finished work early."

"You already knew this about me," replied Brad, "I can't always commit to a time, and getting together sometimes would be a spur-of-the-moment thing."

"I do know that, but it doesn't necessarily mean I have to drop everything when you call," she said abruptly, and a little upset with his insensitivity.

"I'm not even sure why you're doing his editing?" continued Brad. "He's not paying you, it's your time, and time is money!"

"To you maybe, but not to me," she replied wanting to hang up. "I have never done this before, it's a once in a lifetime opportunity, and I'm also finding out a lot about myself."

"Like what?" he asked sharply.

"Like how much I enjoyed editing! How good I am at it! How much fun it is!" she snapped back. "There is no price I could put on that." She was now upset.

Brad was silent.

"I have to go make dinner," she said, deciding she had enough.

"You're always with him," said Brad. It was starting to bother him.

"Michael is helping me out with Ava, which is helping me catch up on my bills," she replied. She was angry but took a second to cool down. "Of course I see a lot of him, he watches Ava here." Although she knew Brad wasn't referring to that.

Brad recognized he had said the wrong thing and quickly changed the subject. "Emily I'm sorry," he said without meaning it, Michael was now becoming a mood point. "Work has been busy, I'm stressed, and tired," he explained, looking for her sympathy. "I just wanted to see you, that's all." Which he did, but only because his business dinner had been canceled at the last minute.

"I have to go," she said coldly, and not believing him, "goodbye." Emily hung up without hearing his response.

Text to Michael: "Loving it more and more. I think you have something incredibly special here."

Michael: "Thanks, can't wait to see your suggestions."

Emily: "You mean my irrefutable edits!"

Michael: "Okay, okay, your irrefutable edits."

Emily: "That's more like it."

Michael: "You're up late, it's almost midnight."

Emily: "I can't put it down, another hour then bed, I promise."

Michael: "It's not like you need any beauty sleep."

Emily: "Thank you, you say the nicest things." She was blushing.

Michael: "Night."

Emily: "Night." She put her phone down, edited for another hour, and then fell asleep.

Chapter 17

"Where are you guys?" Emily yelled as she closed the front door.

"In the kitchen," Ava shouted back.

"Oh, it smells good," she said joining them at the stove.

"We made spaghetti and meatballs for dinner, with garlic bread and cheese," replied Ava with a cheery face.

Michael passed Emily a glass of wine. "Upstairs, change, dinner will be ready in…" he said glancing over "Chef Ava?"

"Five minutes," she confirmed.

When Emily returned the bowls of pasta were being placed on the table. "This looks delightful," she said sitting down.

As they ate, Ava talked about school, Emily about work, and Michael told a funny story about a dog chasing him down the street. After dinner they went into the living room, watched Christmas cartoons, and an hour later Emily put Ava to bed.

"She will be asleep in no time," said Emily flopping herself next to Michael.

Michael filled up her wine glass "I meant to tell you during dinner Bob called me today."

"He did," she said sitting up attentively. "What did he want?"

"Apparently his publisher friend, his name is Peter Paterson, said one of the novels they were planning on publishing fell through. Bob didn't tell me the reason why, but they need to find a replacement quickly, and already have two they are strongly considering. Bob said if I can get mine to Peter this weekend, it will give them a couple of weeks to review it and will take mine into consideration. Peter wants to decide by December twenty-third, and have a contract signed by the end of the year."

"That is amazing!" she said excitedly squeezing his hand. "I have more good news for you. I will be finished my editing Thursday evening."

"That's great news!"

"I will come by your place Friday morning, we can review it, you can update it, and then send it off."

"That means I can send it to Peter Friday afternoon, which will give him his two-week window," said Michael cheerfully.

"I'm so happy for you," she said animatedly.

"Thank you for editing it for me, I feel a lot more comfortable sending it, knowing you did."

"You haven't even seen the edits yet," she suggested mischievously pushing him.

"I know I haven't, but I can tell by your enthusiasm and confident, I won't be disappointed."

"You're right I am enthusiastic and confident about what I have done," she replied proudly, then sipped her wine, and looked at him. "Can I ask you a personal question?"

"Of course, you can."

"Now, if you don't want to answer I understand," she stated warily.

"Okay."

"Why are you single?" It was a question that had been on her mind for some time. "Just haven't met the right girl, huh?" she teased. "Or did someone break your heart?"

"It's a little of both," he said quietly.

"Oh, I am so sorry, I didn't mean to make light of it," Emily said giving him a compassionate look.

"No, don't worry about it, it was a while ago, and her name was Lauren," he said, collecting his thoughts. "Let me go back to the beginning…Before I finished college, I always saw myself as being a writer, but reality being what it is you also need to make money to live. After I graduated, a friend told me that his company was hiring in the city. It was an entry level position with okay pay. So I applied, was offered the job, and accepted. My plan was, I would work during the day and write my novel at night. Then when I made it big, quit my job to write fulltime, and fulfill my dream. Unfortunately, that's all it ever was, a dream. I never found the time to write, no, that's inaccurate. I never made the time to write. Instead, I made excuses up: I'm too tired; I need to go out with my friends; I want to enjoy being single. During this time, I was also successful at the company and quickly moved up the ranks, but as my pay increased, so did my hours at work. I found myself in a situation where I was exceptionally good at what I did; but wasn't happy doing it. I quickly started to dread the train ride to work and back, and going into the office became a chore. I needed to do something I enjoyed, which was writing. So I decided one day to start saving up, that was it, that was my plan. I wasn't sure why or what for, but at least it was a start." Michael took a sip of his wine. "I met Lauren, not this summer, the one before at a party and we hit it off straight away and started dating."

"What clicked?"

"Lauren had graduated with a business degree, worked for a big company in the city similar to mine, I guess in a way, we had followed the same path and had common ground work-wise."

"Was she good looking?"

"She was an attractive blonde…" he stopped and glanced at her, "shall I tell you all the things I told her, you know what a girl likes to hear, or shall I stop there,"

Emily laughed and smacked his arm. "Getting me back for Brad, I see."

"Who me? Never," replied Michael with a cheeky grin.

"To answer your question, yes, please stop there," replied Emily. "Although I would like to hear what she was like?"

"Well Lauren was quite ambitious, driven, and outgoing. She loved to socialize, go to restaurants, and the theatre. Which I liked about her. She would joke about how we would both move up the corporate ladder, and how successful and rich we would be one day. Unfortunately, in my heart I knew that wasn't the life I wanted."

"Did she know how you felt?"

"No, I never told her."

"Why not?"

"She said she was only joking, plus I really didn't have any other plans, or anything concrete to tell her," he said drinking his wine. "A lot of people, besides me, don't like their jobs but still have to show up every day."

"Here, here," agreed Emily lifting up her glass and taking a long drink of her wine.

"After a while it dawned on me, when Lauren talked about us moving up the ladder and being successful and rich, she wasn't joking. It was at that point I became unsure about us."

"In what way?"

"Simply put, she was heading in a different direction than me. I didn't want to be a successful businessperson like she did, I wanted to be a writer, and that would be the only work that would make me happy."

"I understand."

"Late fall, my great-aunt Carol took sick, and they had to move her to a nursing home, my great-uncle Paul had died a few years earlier. Since they couldn't have children, and we were the only family she had, we would all take turns going to visit her. Which meant I usually went every other week for a few hours. One time I was with her, she was sitting up in her bed and usually I would sit in a chair next to her while watching television, except this time she asked me to turn the TV off and sit on the edge of the bed. She told me she wanted to talk to me. I did what she asked, and when I sat down, she stared at me for a long time then said everyone who visited her had happiness in their eyes. My sister, her husband, my parents, even my cousins, but not me. She told me when she looked deep into my eyes, she saw sadness, and then asked me why I was sad. At first, I was going to lie and tell her I was fine, but I couldn't. So, I told her the reason why I was unhappy. Then she asked me about Lauren, after I answered her, she tells me Lauren wasn't the right girl for me. I asked her why she thought that, and she said to me if Lauren loves you, she will support you and your dream. And if you don't follow your dream, you will regret it for the rest of your life. I asked her what if I fail. She said no one had ever been called a failure for trying to make their dream come true. Then she gave me another long look and asked me, 'would you prefer to try and fail; then to have never tried at all.'"

"Wow, she's seems very wise and philosophical."

"Yeah, it's one of the things I loved about her, she would always have these amazing quotes and cool lines."

"What happened next?" she asked, loving his stories.

"After I left her, I started to think to think about what she had said more and more. I also thought about Bea, Bob, and how disappointed they would be with me for not writing. But more importantly, I was most disappointed with myself for not following my dream. Honestly, I felt like I had sold myself out."

"What did you do?"

"About five weeks before Christmas I made a decision. I went to Lauren's apartment, before she came home, and made a special dinner. Lauren was all excited as we ate and drank champagne, she said she knew I had something important to tell her, so I asked her to guess. What did you think she said?" he asked looking at Emily.

"She said you got a promotion."

Michael sat back. "How did you know?" he asked impressed.

"She talked about you two climbing the corporate ladder, you made a special meal and bought champagne, and she knew you were celebrating something," said Emily staring into his eyes. "But you weren't celebrating your promotion, were you?"

"No, I wasn't," he replied softly. "I proceeded to tell Lauren I had given my two-week notice at work and was going to use my savings to support myself while I wrote my novel. She didn't take it well, in fact she told me she didn't want to be dating an unsuccessful penniless writer, and that—"

"Penniless writer?"

"It's what snobby businesspeople refer to those people trying to be successful in the arts. They call them a penniless writer, a penniless musician, and so on. After they call someone that, and realize they were hurtful, they try to take it back by saying—"

"By saying it was a reference to the movies, 'you know a penniless writer trying to publish their first big novel.'"

"You've heard it before?"

She shook her head sadly. "Unfortunately, I have."

"Well, when Lauren said it, she never took it back, needless to say that was the end of Lauren and me."

"I don't understand?" she said with a puzzled look. "You had money to support yourself."

"Lauren didn't want to be dating someone like me, or worse, have to explain me to her colleagues and friends. She knew they would all assume she was supporting me and talk about it behind her back. I would be an unwelcome stigma in her life."

"She offered you no support?"

"None whatsoever," he replied.

"You went through all that effort to arrange a special evening; you must have thought she was going to support you?"

"To be honest with you, I did, I thought she was better than that and cared about me."

"She hurt you."

"No, she hurt me a lot."

Emily held his hand, and Michael felt much needed comfort in that simple gesture.

"She broke up with me that night and I never saw her again."

"Do you know what happened to her?"

"After last Christmas, I heard she received a big promotion, and moved to California."

"What did you do?"

"I was upset for a while about the breakup. But once I realized I would never have to take the train, walk through those office doors again, and I was going to write, I became pretty excited. I couldn't wait to start," he explained. "Looking back, I guess it worked out best for the both of us in the end."

"Things happen for a reason," suggested Emily.

"They do," agreed Michael.

"What about your great-aunt?"

"The next time I visited her she made me sit on the bed again, so I knew she wanted to talk some more. As soon as she looked into my eyes, she said, 'you have beautiful happy eyes, and I know you made a decision to follow your dream; you are going to be a writer.' I told her I was, and was about to tell her about Lauren, but before I could, she told me Lauren had left me to follow her own dream."

"She said that!" said Emily surprised.

"Don't ask me how she knew," said Michael shaking his head. "Then I told my great-aunt I was staying with my parents over Christmas and in the new year finding my own place, which is where I live today."

"How long will your savings last?"

"Another two years," he confirmed.

"When did you move into your apartment?" she asked wanting to hear the end of his story.

"I moved in February first, started my novel at the end of February, and spent the next nine months writing. I finished my manuscript on the same day I met you."

"The best day of your life!" said Emily with a confident smile.

"Yeah, it was," he said leaning back with a grin and placing his hands over his head, "the day I finished my manuscript."

"Hey, mister! You knew what I meant!" she said tickling him under the arms.

"I give in, I give in," he said laughing and trying to wiggle away from her but falling on the floor. As he did, he gently grabbed her, and pulled her on top of him. She was inches from his face. Kiss her, he thought, just kiss her.

If he kisses me, she thought, I will definitely kiss him back.

Michael knew he shouldn't, instead, he tickled her till she moved next to him on the floor then quickly stood up. "It's late, I need to get going, and you still have editing to do tonight, Ms.," he said reaching out his hand.

"I do," replied Emily as she held it, was pulled up, and gave him a delightful smile. "I'll be home around five tomorrow."

"Yes, I know, I dread that more than walking through my old office doors," joked Michael as he put on his coat.

"Hey, thanks a lot!" she said playfully pushing him. "Admit it? You like seeing me! Come on, admit it?"

"Maybe."

"Did you just say, maybe?" she asked, walking to the door, and opening it. "You may leave now," she said pointing outside.

Michael walked out, turned around, and smiled. "Goodnight."

"Goodnight," she replied, then stuck her head out the door, and watched him till he was out of sight. She closed the door and smiled, then turned off the lights, and went upstairs to edit his manuscript.

Chapter 18

"What's for dinner?" asked Emily walking into the kitchen.

"We made lasagna, well we didn't make it, it was frozen in a box, we just put it in the oven," clarified Ava. "We did make the salad though."

"It looks delicious," said Emily looking at it.

"How was work?" asked Michael.

"It was busy," she replied. "It's nice to be home."

"Dinner will be about ten minutes."

"I'm going to change straight into my pajamas," said Emily heading for the stairs.

"Me too," cried Ava chasing after her.

After dinner Michael hung around for a while, leaving around seven. Emily played with Ava for an hour before turning everything off, putting Ava to bed, and going into her room. She grabbed the binder, lay on her bed, and started to edit; three hours later she was finished. She smiled to herself at what she had accomplished and was looking forward to seeing Michael's reaction tomorrow morning. Most of her free time these last couple of weeks had been spent editing his novel, usually nights at home or lunch breaks during work; how exciting and rewarding it had been. But now, for some reason, she was sad. As Emily got off her bed, placed the binder in the bag and crawled under her sheets, she wondered why. Then it came to her, once she had reviewed it with Michael tomorrow, her editing was done.

Chapter 19

"Good morning, Michael," said Emily strolling through his front door.

"Good morning."

"I picked up coffees and bagels for us," she said balancing them and the bag containing the manuscript.

"Here, let me help with something," said Michael taking the coffees and putting them on the dining room table. "Why don't we review it here," he suggested as he watched Emily put down the bagels, take the two binders out of the bag, and place them next to the coffees.

"When are you going to put up your Christmas decorations?" she asked looking around.

"I didn't want to say anything in front of Ava because I wanted to ask you first," said Michael. "On the twenty-third my niece and two nephews are coming here for the night. I'm going to help them make decorations and let them garnish my house. I thought Ava may want to come?"

"Oh, she would love that!"

"Great, Jenny will be so excited having a girl to decorate with."

"That'll be so much fun for the both of them. Ava has been wanting to meet Jenny ever since you mentioned her," said Emily picking up a coffee and taking a sip. "I should see if someone wants that night off at work and pick up another shift."

"You should," said Michael nodding in agreement. "My parents, sister, and her husband, are going to be wrapping presents at my parent's place that night, and the next day after lunch I'm either taking the kids to my parents or my family is coming here," explained Michael. "I think you're working Christmas Eve?"

"Yeah, we're closing early though, I will be out the door by five."

"Maybe Ava can stay here with us," he suggested.

"That sounds ideal," said Emily relieved. "It will be comforting to know she will be with you and your family and having a good time playing with Jenny and your nephews."

"She'll have a great time," said Michael reassuring her. "I'll let you know the details closer to the day."

"Okay," she replied sitting and opening up the first binder. "Shall we get started?"

They spent the next couple of hours going through her edits, and when they finished, Michael sat back in his chair and looked at her in amazement.

"What?" she asked with a big grin.

"You know what!" he replied with a smile. "This is brilliant!"

"You think so!" she asked unsure.

"No, I don't think so, I know so!" he said pulling her up from the chair gave and giving her a big hug. "Thank you."

Emily went flush. She liked the feel of his arms around her and didn't want him to let go.

Eventually he pulled away and they sat down. "Now, I also have to send in a query letter and synopsis which I have over here," said Michael walking over to the printer. "Do you think you can give them a once over for me?"

"Of course," said Emily picking up her pen and spending the next fifteen minutes editing them. "Maybe change this here…this…this…and this," she suggested as she reviewed them with him.

"Will do," agreed Michael.

"Then you're good to go."

"You know, you were right," he said looking at her.

"Really, about what?"

"That I would agree to all your edits," he said gently holding her hand. "I am so happy for you, that was an excellent job, and you should be very proud."

"I am, thank you," she replied confidently. "Now, what's next for you to do?"

"Update the manuscript and these two documents today, Gmail them to the publisher this afternoon, and then I wait, I wait, and I wait," he said letting go off her hand and pretending to act nervous.

"Oh please! You're so silly," she said giggling at his antics. "You have nothing to worry about. They would be crazy not to publish it. It's a beautiful, well-written piece, and I loved it."

"You're forgetting one thing," he said.

"What's that?" she wondered.

"It also has outstanding, amazing, and professional editing."

Her face went red. "Thank you."

As they drank their coffees, ate their bagels, Emily remembered something she wanted to ask him. "Your great-aunt Carol, you never mentioned what happened to her?"

"She passed way about a week before Christmas. It's almost a year now."

"I'm sorry to hear that," she said sadly.

"You never like to see anyone go, but I have many fond memories of her, and I know she had a long, fulfilling, and happy life," revealed Michael. "I did get to see her a few days before she died."

"Oh, you did, that's nice."

"Actually, she told me this story, do you want to hear it?"

"You know I do!" she replied eagerly. "But first let's get comfy on the couch."

Emily waited for Michael to sit next to her then moved closer to him. "Okay, I'm ready, tell me," she said impatiently.

"When my great-aunt Carol was around eighteen, she fell in love with a young man and they dated close to a year, and right before Christmas he broke up with her. The young man went off, met someone else, and eventually married her. My great-aunt's heart was broken. For the following year she was sad, alone, and believed she would never find true love again. On the anniversary of the breakup, she was sitting on a park bench thinking about the man who left her and began to cry. When she looked up there was this handsome man sitting next to her. He offered her his handkerchief which she accepted to dry her eyes. Then they started talking and she told him what had happened. The man asked her if she wanted to go for a coffee, which she accepted, during which he asked if she wanted to go to the movies the following night, which they did. Then they saw each other the following night."

"Your great-uncle Paul!" said Emily excitedly.

"Yes, it was my great-uncle Paul," replied Michael smiling at her enthusiasm. "On Christmas Eve, he asked her into the parlor for some privacy, because he wanted to give her a Christmas present. She unwrapped the present, opened the small box, and inside was a thin gold band ring with a small teardrop diamond setting," explained Michael. "Now, it wasn't an engagement ring because they had only known each other for a couple of weeks, so he places it on the middle finger of her right hand and when he does, he promises her that from this day forward the only tears she will cry will be tears of happiness. From that point on, my great-aunt Carol affectionately named the ring, 'The Christmas Teardrop,' and from the day he put it on until the day she passed, she never took that ring off. And while he was alive, my great-uncle Paul kept his promise."

"Oh, that is so romantic," said Emily as her eyes started to well up. "I love this story!"

"Wait, there's more."

"Tell me! Tell me!" said Emily pulling on his arm.

"The day of her funeral she had an open casket. When I went up to pay my respects, my great-aunt had her hands crossed holding a rosary, and the ring wasn't on her finger."

"Someone took it!" said Emily horrified, "I can't believe it!"

"I thought that too and decided not to mention it to my mother till after the funeral. We are at the cemetery, the service is finished, and my mother asks me to go for a walk with her, so I do. She stops, looks at me, and gives me a small box. I open it up and—"

"It's the ring!" said Emily.

"Yes, it's the ring," said Michael. "My mom tells me, my great-aunt Carol had given the ring to my mom, to give to me."

"She wanted you to have it?"

"She did," replied Michael. "My great-aunt told my mom, and these are her words, 'do not give it to Michael until I'm six feet under, that way he can't give it back to me.'"

Emily couldn't help but laugh. "That is funny."

"I know, my mom and I laughed when she told me too, but that was my great-aunt Carol," said Michael. "Along with the ring there was a note, my mom told me Great-Aunt Carol was too weak to write it, so my mom wrote if for her, but she insisted on signing it. My mom moved off to the side to let me read it in private."

"Oh, what did it say?" she asked in a melancholy voice.

"It read, 'Dearest Michael, one day you will find a very special woman whom you will give your heart to unconditionally, and in return, she will give you hers. Always remember to love and support one another through the good times, but more importantly, the not so good times. And promise her, what your great-uncle Paul promised me, and you both will be filled with happiness, forever, God Bless, Love Great-Aunt Carol.'"

"That is so beautiful," said Emily wiping her eyes.

"Shall I stop," teased Michael.

"Not a chance mister, you continue."

"I walked over to my mom, put my arm through hers, and we started walking back to the family. On the way, my mom tells me Great-Aunt Carol had given the ring to the right person, and besides her and my dad, I was the only one who knew the story of, 'The Christmas Teardrop.' She continued by saying that my great-aunt Carol hoped one day I would use it in one of my novels and share her story with the world."

"It is such a lovely story," said Emily. "Are you going to use it?"

"In my next novel I think I will," he said giving Emily a peculiar look.

"What? Why are you are looking at me like that?"

"Do you want to see it?"

"You have it here?" she asked ecstatically.

"I do."

"Yes, yes, show me, show me!"

She watched Michael go into his bedroom, come out with a ring box, open it, and pass it to her. "Oh my! This is the most beautiful ring I have ever seen! It is so elegant, so perfect!"

"I believe she wanted me to use it as an engagement ring," said Michael hesitantly, "but I think girls today want to pick their own."

"No, not me," said Emily emphatically. "I would love to have a ring like this. It has history, it has a romantic story, and it's been passed on to you, so now it has tradition. I think if the girl you decided to marry doesn't want this ring you have picked the wrong girl," she said closing the box and handing it back to him. "I think your great-aunt Carol and mom are right, she did give it to the right person."

"Thank you," he replied quietly, placing the box on the coffee table.

"You know what I love about you." Realizing what she said, she quickly corrected herself. "Your stories…I mean, what I love about you are your stories, and the way you tell them. I feel like I am right there with the characters watching the plot unfold."

"I love, that you love them," he said playing on her words.

"Ha, ha, very funny," she responded smiling at his wordplay. "What am I going to do with you?" she asked shaking her head.

He innocently looked upon her.

"The innocent thing isn't working," she said chuckling and standing, although she did think it was extremely cute. "I should go and let you start working on these documents or you will miss your deadline. Plus, I need to get groceries, Ava said you guys want to make pizzas for dinner?"

"We do," he verified, "and we will try not to burn the house down."

"That would be greatly appreciated," she admitted putting on her coat. "You know I'm going to be very late tonight, if you want, you can crash on the couch?"

"Maybe I will," replied Michael considering it.

Emily started to the door. "I was going to mention this before I went to work tonight, maybe it's best I ask you now, so you can bring a change of clothes. I haven't told Ava yet so don't say anything, but I'm taking her to see Santa at the mall tomorrow, do you want to come with us?"

"Sure, I would like that."

"Great, I'll see you later on this afternoon, around four thirty."

"Four thirty," he confirmed. "Thanks again for editing my manuscript you did an incredible job."

"You are very welcome," she said cheerfully. "Bye."

"Bye," he replied closing the door behind her. He looked over at the ring box on the coffee table, picked it up, and put it back in his bedroom.

Chapter 20

Emily went outside to get the last of the groceries then closed the car door.

"Emily!" shouted a voice from behind.

She turned around as Brad walked up to her.

"These are for you," he said as he took the grocery bag from her and handed her a dozen red roses.

"These are beautiful," she said admiring them.

"Like my, Emily," he replied and followed her into the house.

"I don't have long, my flight leaves soon, I just wanted to drop the roses off and this," he said handing her a big envelope.

"What's this?" she asked looking at it.

"Open it and see," he said cheerfully.

She opened it up and took out its contents. "It's a registration form and information package on the journalism program at the college."

"I thought you may want to look it over, see what they offer, and what you think about it," he said eagerly.

"Thanks, that's so thoughtful of you, I will."

"How is your editing going?" he asked trying his best to sound interested.

"I finished it last night and gave it back to him this morning he—"

"Awesome, that means when I get back on Thursday, you will have some time for me," he said with a cunning grin. "Let's say, dinner?"

"I guess."

"He looked at the time, I have to run, I'll talk to you soon," he said leaving as quickly as he came.

Emily put the documents back in the envelope and placed it on the kitchen counter. She looked at the roses and contemplated throwing them out; instead, she put them in a vase, and put the vase in her bedroom out of sight. She picked up Ava from the bus stop and played with her for a while until Michael showed up then got ready for work, said goodbye, and left. At two thirty she quietly walked in trying not to wake Michael.

"How was work?" he whispered.

"I'm sorry. Did I wake you?" she whispered back.

"No, you can put the light on."

She turned it on, took off her coat, and watched as Michael moved his feet. She collapsed on the couch. "What a night, busy, busy, busy!"

"Come here," he said pulling her next to him, as he held her in his arms she snuggled into his chest.

"This is so cozy and you're so warm," she said and drifted off to sleep.

Chapter 21

"Mommy, wake up," said Ava shaking her. "Why are you sleeping on the couch?"

Emily woke up in a panic, fearing she was lying next to Michael, but was relieved when she realized she was alone. "I laid down for a minute last night when I came home, I must have fallen asleep. Mommy had a busy night last night, honey," she explained as Ava cuddled next to her. "Do you want to do something fun today? Do you want to go the mall and see…Santa?"

"Yes, I do! I do! Let's get ready," she said looking around and noticing something. "Where's Michael? Last night he said he may be sleeping over."

Emily wasn't sure either.

"Maybe he wants to come?"

"I know he does," replied Emily still trying to figure out what had happened to him. Her train of thought was disrupted by a knock on the door.

"I'll get it," said Ava jumping up and unlocking it. "Michael!" she yelled joyfully. "Mom it's Michael," she said jumping back on the couch next to her.

"I hope I didn't wake you guys up," he said apologetically and closing the door.

"No, we woke up five minutes ago," answered Ava. "Where did you go?"

A question on Emily's mind too.

"Your mom came home, I was talking to her on the couch, and the next minute all I hear is her snoring," he replied imitating her which made them laugh. "So, I put a blanket over her and tiptoed out of here," he said showing Ava how he did it.

Ava jumped off the couch. "Next time, do it like this," she said, slouching, curving her hands in front of her face, and creeping on her tiptoes.

"Like this," said Michael trying to copy her.

Ava broke into a hysterical laugh and deliberately fell over the couch onto her mom. Her mom started tickling her, making her laugh louder. "Okay, miss, upstairs, and brush your teeth."

"Do you want to help me make pancakes?" asked Michael as he watched Ava stand up.

"Pancakes! Definitely!"

"Then hurry up and brush those teeth," he said as he watched her takeoff up the stairs before sitting on the couch next to Emily. "How are you doing this morning? Still tired?"

"A little, I'll be okay after I have a coffee," she said glancing over at him. "What did happen last night?"

"You fell asleep, then I did, luckily you let out this big snore which woke me up."

"I did not."

"I'm afraid you did, around six this morning," he confirmed. "I thought I better head home before Ava woke up. So, I put a blanket over you and left."

"Thank you for that, after Ava woke me, I had this dreadful fear you were lying next to me."

"Oh really, I'm your dreadful fear, am I?"

"No, nothing can be furthest from the truth," she said wanting to pull him next to her for a quick cuddle.

"Well, I'm glad to hear that," he said jumping to his feet. "Let me make you a coffee, which you can take upstairs with you, while Chef Ava and I make chocolate chip pancakes."

With coffee in hand, she passed Ava sprinting down the stairs, went into her room, and laid a pretty red dress on her bed. As she was washing her hair in the shower, Emily thought about Michael holding her in his arms. How cozy and warm he was, and how safe and secure she felt, snuggled into him. It was a feeling she had never felt before and she liked it, actually, she liked it a lot. When she came downstairs the pancakes were done and the kitchen was a mess. Ava had batter in her hair, on her face, and chocolate all around her mouth. They both smiled guiltily and pointed at one another. She laughed at them and told them to wait while she took their picture. After she did, they sat, ate pancakes, and Emily listened to Ava and Michael blame one other for the mess.

"Okay, Ava, upstairs for a shower," said Emily standing.

"Oh mom, five more minutes," she pleaded.

"Five more minutes, perfect, that means you can help me clean up," suggested Michael teasingly.

"Ah!" screamed Ava as she took off for the stairs.

Emily watched her and shook her head. "She's quite the actress!" she said turning to Michael. "Do you want me to help you?"

"No, I got it."

"Okay, I'm going to go upstairs and help Ava get ready," said Emily. "We won't be long."

"Go ahead, I'll be finished by the time you both come down," replied Michael picking up the dirty dishes.

"You're the best," she said appreciatively, before going upstairs.

Chapter 22

They arrived at the mall and waited in line for Santa. When it was Ava's turn, she told him what she wanted, and smiled for her picture. Once it was printed, she put it in her bag. Then they walked around the mall, going into all the stores that sold toys, and watched Ava pointing out the ones she had on her list and why she just had to have them.

"I love looking at all the people busily shopping for loved ones, feeling the Christmas spirit in the air, and how magical it all is," said Emily as they sat at a table in the food court.

"It truly is," agreed Michael looking around.

"Can we get my snack now?" asked Ava "I'm starving."

"There's a mood killer," joked Emily laughing.

"Let's go, Ava," said Michael chuckling at Emily's comment, "first your snack, then coffee for me and your mom."

As they stood up to leave Emily's phone rang and she answered it. "You can take her but I'm not at home, I'm at the mall," she said, and then listened. "You're here also?" she repeated, "Where are you?" Emily listened again. "So are we!" Emily stood up and started looking around. "Where are you?" she asked looking at Ava, "Grandma and Granddad are here at the mall, somewhere in the food court." She watched as Ava stood on her chair and excitedly looked for them. "You're by the restrooms. Oh, I see you! Turn around, I'm waving." She watched as they waved back and started to head towards her. Emily pointed them out to Ava who ran off to meet them. In the distance, she watched as Ava hugged them, and walked them to their table.

"Hi, Mom, Dad," she said giving them a hug. "I didn't know you would be here today."

"We were hoping to pick Ava up from your place, we couldn't get a hold of you, so we thought we would walk around her till we did," replied her mother.

"I'm only here to carry the bags," added her father lifting them up.

Emily noticed her mom looking at Michael. "How rude of me! Mom, Dad, this is my friend Michael, Michael, my parents."

"Hello, Michael, Isabelle, glad to meet you."

"Hello, Michael, I'm John."

"Isabelle, John, nice to meet you both," he replied shaking their hands.

After they sat, Michael went with Ava to get her fries and a coke, and the adults' coffees. When they returned, they sat and listened as Emily updated her parents on meeting Michael, editing his book, working more hours, and how he was helping her with Ava. Brad's name never came up.

"Looks like you have a good friend there," commented Isabelle as she looked over at Michael.

"He's a great friend, the best," said Emily squeezing his arm.

Her parents noticed her affection and quickly glanced at one another.

Emily looked at Michael. "I meant to ask you last night, then this morning in the shower..." She stopped, glanced at her parents, and corrected herself. "I was in the shower alone, he was downstairs making pancakes with Ava, I was thinking in the shower about him and my question," she said and was blushing more now, because in correcting herself by saying they weren't in the shower together, she had inadvertently told them she was thinking about him, while in the shower. Her parents just smiled, and she wondered what they were thinking. Just ask the question quickly, she thought to herself. "Michael, did you Gmail the documents to the publisher?"

Michael tried not to chuckle at her red face. "I did, I sent them out yesterday afternoon, and he verified he had received them."

"It's so exciting and I'm so happy for you," said Emily as her parents looked on at her. She realized it may be time to quit, while not ahead, and went quiet.

Michael noticed her body language and took over the conversation. "Your daughter is an excellent editor, you should be very proud of her, she did an amazing job with my manuscript."

"She has always been excellent at editing," praised her father. "She used to write some good stories, too."

"I didn't know she liked to write also," said Michael surprised and glancing over at her.

"I did do some writing," she replied shyly, "but I preferred editing more."

"Isabelle, I think we still have her old stories at home, don't we?"

"Yes, dear, in her bedroom closet, along with her college stuff."

"I will look for them when I get home," validated John. "I'll drop them off, you can have a read of them Michael, and let her know what you think."

"That's okay, Dad," replied Emily wanting to sink under the table. "I'm sure Michael doesn't want to be bothered reading them."

"On the contrary," said Michael laughing inside at the word he had just used, and the look Emily was giving him. But he quickly felt sorry for her and turned to her dad. "I would like that John, as long as Emily doesn't mind?" he asked glancing over at Emily, but her mom interjected.

"Of course she wouldn't mind, besides she read yours, right Emily?"

They were all looking at her. "No, I don't mind," she replied awkwardly.

"Ava, where's your picture with Santa?" asked Michael changing the subject.

Ava showed them the picture and talked about the presents she wanted from him. Then the adults talked about the mall being busy and Christmas. It was getting late, so they said their goodbyes. Isabelle, John, and Ava went one way, while Emily and Michael went the other.

"I didn't know you wrote?"

"I had to as part of my college program."

"That's it?" he asked inquisitively.

"Okay, okay, the ones my father is talking about are personal ones I wrote," she confessed.

"You really don't mind me reading them?"

"On the contrary!" she replied.

They both laughed out loud.

"You're something else," said Emily. "I don't know why I put up with you?"

"My irresistible charm?" he quipped.

"Oh please, you're making me nauseous," she replied, although he was extremely charming. "Back at the table I was horrified at the idea of you reading my stories, but actually, I would like you to," she said putting her arm through his. "I would love to hear your thoughts on them."

"Then I will," he confirmed as they walked towards the exit. "Do you like editing more?"

"Don't get me wrong, I like writing because you can use your imagination to create a setting, develop your characters, structure the main plot, and sub plots. Basically, you create your own little world and allow your readers to escape to it with you," she explained. "But I just enjoy editing more. I like making what has been written, perfect, so the writer can feel confident with his work and know their reader has a seamless piece of literature to revel in."

"Thanks to you, I am very confident my work is seamless," he said praising her.

She pulled him close as they went outside in the cold. They got into her car and started for home. "I'm meeting Sue in thirty minutes before work to have a chat, you know, catch up on this week's gossip," she explained. "You have a free night now. What are you going to do?"

"I don't know, I haven't had time to think about it."

"I'm first off at work tonight and I should be finished around nine thirty. Do you want to do something together? Maybe go out somewhere?"

"I wouldn't mind getting out, it's been a while."

"Do you like playing pool?"

"I do."

"Me too," she said quickly looking at him. "There's a bar ten minutes from where I work that has a pool table, we can go there?"

"Perfect."

"I wouldn't mind going home first and getting changed," she said. "I can text you when I'm leaving work and we can meet at my place."

"It's a da—" he said stopping himself midway through the word 'date.' "Sure."

Chapter 23

"So, what's the latest," asked Sue sipping her coffee.

Emily started by telling her about talking with Michael on Monday about how she met Brad. "I got the feeling that Michael isn't too fond of Brad."

"Why is that?"

"He made me feel like Brad tricked me into making me feel sorry for him because I didn't want to work at his friend's restaurant and that's why I went out with him again. I didn't want to say anything to Michael, but the more I think about it, the more I think he's right. What do you think?"

"You know as well as I do, Brad is one hell of a salesman, and he knows how to work situations to his advantage," said Sue. "That guy can sell ice to polar bears!"

"I know," replied Emily, a little upset she had been duped. Then she told Sue about Brad's conversation with her on Tuesday evening and what he said.

"He has some nerve, not only putting Michael down for helping you with Ava but you also, for not taking any money from him and editing for the experience."

"He tried to apologize but I don't think he meant it."

Sue believed Emily was right, so she didn't respond to her, instead, she changed the subject. "Anything interesting happen Wednesday?"

Emily told her about Ava and Michael making her spaghetti and meatballs, watching Christmas cartoons, and about the publisher asking Michael to send in his manuscript. Then she then told her about Lauren.

Sue shuddered. "She sounds like one cold, shallow, you know what!"

"I know, I felt sorry for him, she really hurt him," said Emily. "But I think he feels that what happened worked out best for the both of them in the end."

"And for you too, by the looks of it," said Sue matter-of-fact.

"What do you mean by that?" she queried.

"Well, you have a great friend, and your daughter has a good male role model," replied Sue. It was partially what she meant; besides, she didn't want to tell her everything, sometimes friends just need to figure out some things on their own.

"Oh, I see what you mean," said Emily, knowing Sue meant something else, but wasn't going to ask her what.

"So, Michael saved up money, quit his job to write, and is living off that," summarized Sue. "How long till his money runs dry?"

"About two years."

"Then what?"

"I don't know, I guess he will worry about that when he gets there."

"If he doesn't publish any books, he will have lots to worry about when he gets there," said Sue candidly.

"Sue, his novel is beautiful," she said in his defense, "I know it will get published, he's extremely talented."

Sue knew what Emily was doing and smiled to herself.

"On Friday morning, I went over, and we reviewed my edited manuscript. He said it was brilliant, amazing, impressive, and professional. Thank you very much," she said playfully patting herself on the back, "and, he kept all my edits."

"I'm proud of you Emily, and you should be too," said Sue congratulating her, "here let me do that," and took over patting Emily on the back.

Emily purposely omitted telling Sue about his great-aunt Carol and 'The Christmas Teardrop,' instead, going straight to Brad showing up with roses, and information package on the journalism program at the college.

"That guy is one smooth operator," said Sue shaking her head, "he doesn't miss a beat."

"I think the roses were part of his apology and the college information was to show me what he can offer. I don't know, I guess he means well."

"I'm sure he has your best interests at heart, honey," said Sue comfortingly.

"I guess," replied Emily, then gave Sue a look that she picked up on straight away.

"Oh, you have something good for me?" asked Sue wanting to hear what it was. "Come on, tell me!"

She told her about getting home late after work and snuggling with Michael on the couch.

"You never?" asked Sue.

"I did."

"Did Ava see you two the next morning?"

"No, he left before she woke up, he said he didn't want her to see us," replied Emily. "Isn't that sweet."

"That is a gentleman you have there, hands down!"

Then Emily told her about the mall and her parents.

"You introduced him to your parents?"

"Well, yes," she replied, "but not intentionally though, they just happened to be there. I told them he was my good friend."

"They're buying into that, too?"

"Well, yeah, maybe, until I—"

"I know this is going to be a gem, let's hear it!"

Emily told Sue about the shower.

Sue laughed loudly. "Girl, you put yourself in a bad spot there."

"Luckily Michael came to my rescue and changed the subject," she said sipping her coffee. "Now you're all caught up."

Sue looked at Emily for a while then grinned. "Since I have known you, I have never seen you so happy."

"Is it that noticeable?"

"Like day and night," she said, "like day and night." Sue gently touched Emily's arm. "I'll tell you these coffee talks are a thousand percent more enjoyable since Michael came onto the scene."

"You're right, they are," said Emily with a smile.

"In fact, I actually look forward to them now," she said half-joking, and waited for her reaction.

"Sue!"

Chapter 24

Emily: "Leaving work now, be home in ten minutes, I'll text you when I'm home."

Michael: "Okay."

Emily: "Home, getting a shower, will leave front door unlocked, help yourself to a beer."

Michael: "On my way."

Michael opened the door, walked in, and hung up his coat. The tree lights were on, Christmas music was playing, and upstairs he could hear the shower running. He took a beer from the fridge and sat on the couch. Twenty minutes later Emily walked into the room. Her hair was straight and past her shoulders, she had on a little makeup, and red lipstick. She was wearing a light, fitted sweater, with tight jeans tucked into knee-high boots.

"Wow, you look incredible!" said Michael.

"Thank you," she replied as she did a full turn then went into kitchen. When she came out she sat next to Michael and handed him a beer. "I'm looking forward to tonight, I haven't been out for a beer or played pool in a long time."

"Same here."

When they arrived at the bar, they ordered beers, and claimed the pool table. They started to play, but neither of them was particularly good. So they spent most of the time laughing and joking about each other's bad shots and cheered if someone made a good one. After playing for a couple of hours they sat at a table, talked about the music, and watched the people dancing.

"I love this song," said Emily. "Do you want to dance?"

"Sure," replied Michael, and was hypnotized as he watched Emily move her body to the beat. He thought she was beautiful, sexy, and enchanting.

They danced for a few more songs then took a break. Michael grabbed their beers, and Emily followed him outside to the back patio.

"This cool air feels so good," she said as she sat on one of the picnic tables. "I am having so a good time."

"Me too," he said sitting next to her as she moved over close to him. "I haven't had this much fun in a long time," he said nudging her shoulder, "and having a friend as beautiful and sexy as you, doesn't hurt either."

She nudged him back. "And having a friend as handsome and athletic as you, doesn't either."

They talked for a while, looked up at the constellations, then headed back inside to get warm, order another drink, and dance some more before heading home.

"Are you coming in for a nightcap?" asked Emily, arriving at her front door. "I promise I won't bite."

"Oh, that's no fun," replied Michael turning to walk away.

"Well, maybe a little," she teased, as she watched him turn back. "Yay!" she said clapping her hands.

They grabbed a beer, sat on the couch, and talked about his manuscript, about her editing, the stories Emily had written, her friend Sue, and her parents.

"I was wondering what they must have thought when I said, 'I meant to ask you last night, then this morning in the shower," said Emily chuckling. "Do you think they thought we were together that night and the next morning in the shower?"

"I don't think so," he replied. "I believe your recovery, 'I was thinking in the shower about him,' really helped convince them otherwise."

"Oh please, stop!" she pleaded. "I'm so embarrassed about that whole conversation with my parents."

"On the contrary," said Michael, making Emily laugh hysterically.

"I can't believe you used that word. I wanted to laugh so much."

"So did I."

"My parents must think we are crazy?" she said looking at him.

"One thing is for sure; they will never forget the first time you introduced them to me."

"No, they won't," she replied, happy with that thought. She put her head on his shoulder, watched the Christmas lights blinking, and listened to the music for a while. "Do you want to crash on the couch tonight?" she asked with a yawn. "My sister's not dropping Ava off till after three."

"All right," he replied.

Emily gave him sheets and blankets, turned off the tree lights, and the music. Then gave him a hug, thanked him for a lovely night, and went upstairs. Michael stripped to his boxers and T-shirt, set up the sheets and blankets on the couch, and was about to turn off the light and lie down.

"Michael," called Emily from upstairs, "Michael."

Michael went to the bottom of the stairs. "Yes."

"Can you come here for a minute?"

He wasn't sure if he should put his jeans back on or not, but figured boxers are like shorts, so he went to the top of the stairs. "Where are you?"

"In here," said Emily from her bedroom.

He walked up to her door and noticed the light shining inside her room. "Are you okay?"

"Yeah, come in."

He opened the door and walked inside. She was underneath the covers on one side of the bed. "Are you okay?"

"Can you lie with me like the other night and hold me till I fall asleep?"

Michael lay down on top of the duvet, put his head on the pillow, and then put his arm around her. Emily put her head on his chest, whispered thank you, and within minutes was asleep.

Chapter 25

When Emily woke up Michael was gone. She put on a robe, went downstairs, and noticed the sheets and blankets neatly folded on the couch. He must have left, she thought. Suddenly she heard the bathroom door open, and Michael walked out. "You're still here," she said happily.

"Yeah, I woke up ten minutes ago."

"Thanks for holding me last night."

"That's okay," he replied, "you fell asleep pretty quickly."

"Trust me, when I'm on my own I toss and turn for hours before I fall asleep. I guess you have that magic touch, magic man!"

"Do you want magic man to use his magic touch to whip us up breakfast?" he joked.

"No, not today," she replied, "I'm taking you out for breakfast, give me fifteen minutes to get ready."

They walked to the diner, ate breakfast, talked about their night, and agreed they would have to do it again soon. When they finished, they went for a walk around the Town Park, then headed back to her place.

"Thanks for last night, I really needed that," she said standing on the sidewalk outside her house.

"You and me both," he confirmed. "I'll see you around four thirty."

"I'll, see you then."

She watched him walk down the street then turned with a smile as she went inside.

Just after three, Ava walked through the door with Debbie. "Mom, we're here," she yelled. "Where are you?"

"Coming down," she replied from the stairs. "There is my angel come give me a hug."

Ava ran over and held her.

"Did you have a good time?"

"We had so much fun," she said energetically and told her what they did before running upstairs.

"Hey, Deb, how are you doing?"

"Good Emily. You?"

"Busy with work!"

"Mom and Dad were telling me you're taking on more shifts. I guess all that extra money will come in handy?"

"I wish," she said walking into the kitchen, "bills, bills, bills. "Do you want a coffee?"

"I'd love one," replied Debbie following her in. "So?"

Emily turned looking at her. "So, what?"

"So, who is Michael?" she asked. "Mom and Dad said he is wonderful and handsome."

"They did?" asked Emily surprised; her parents tended to be mute when it came to her relationships.

"Yeah, they both took to him."

"Really," said Emily turning away, and grinning. "Well, he's only a friend," she confirmed and turned to give her sister a look of 'nothing more.'

"A friend, huh, nothing more," replied Debbie unconvinced. "Ava thinks the world of him, she is always going on about Michael this, and Michael that."

"I know she does," said Emily as she poured their coffees, "he's a great guy."

Debbie looked around. "Where is he?" she asked gesturing with her head upstairs.

"Nice try!"

"Oh, I see, he left this morning before we got her?" she asked naughtily "Don't worry, your secret is safe with me."

"No...well... actually...he did stay over, but—"

"Come on tell me all the sordid details."

"There are none to tell, he slept on the couch I slept in my bed, we went out for breakfast, and then he went home."

"Friends that's all, really?" asked Debbie a little disappointed.

"Friends," Emily reconfirmed. She noticed the disappointment on Deb's face. "If you stick around till I leave for work, you'll meet him. He's watching Emily tonight," she suggested trying to contain her excitement. Deep down Emily wanted Debbie to meet him.

"Put on another pot of coffee," ribbed Debbie, "I'm staying."

They went into the living room, and Debbie listened to Emily talk about what she had been doing these last couple of weeks and noticed all of them involved Michael.

"And he is helping you out with Ava while you are at work?"

"Yeah, either till I get home from my day shifts or like tonight when I get home from the evening ones."

Something hit Debbie. "Brad is out of the picture?"

"Oh no, I'm still seeing Brad."

Debbie was confused; Emily hadn't mentioned his name. "What have you and Brad been up to?"

Emily told her about the party, the Italian restaurant, and him dropping by.

"Oh, that's nice," replied Debbie somewhat unsure about what her sister was doing.

Noticing Debbie's expression Emily changed the subject and asked her what she had been up to, then about Christmas, and her plans.

The hour flew by, and they were interrupted by a knock at the door. Emily looked at the time. "It's Michael, I have to get ready for work. Can you get the door for me?" she asked and took off upstairs.

The door opened and Michael was surprised by the unfamiliar face. "Hi, I'm Michael."

"Hi, Michael come in, Emily told me you would be coming over, she's just getting ready for work," she explained closing the door behind him. "I'm her sister, Debbie."

"Hi, Debbie, nice to meet you." he said politely shaking her hand.

All of a sudden there was a thunderous noise of little feet running down the stairs, and they both turned to see Ava coming around the corner, "Michael!" she screamed leaping into his arms. "I missed you!"

"I missed you, too. Did you have fun with your grandparents and Debbie?"

"I sure did, me and Aunt Debbie stayed up past twelve last night. She made me promise not to tell Mom, but she didn't say anything about you," she whispered and hugged his neck tightly. "I'm so glad you are here! What are we making tonight?"

"I was thinking, cookies."

"Christmas cookies?" she quizzed.

"You know it."

"I can't wait. I'm going to tell Mom you're here," she said running away.

"I'm pretty sure Emily already knows you, with that welcome," suggested Debbie laughing.

"Definitely," said Michael chuckling.

As they sat, Debbie asked Michael about his book. After he did, he told her about the wonderful job Emily did editing it. Then Debbie talked about herself, her work, and Emily.

"Hey, Michael, I see you met Deb."

"Yes, she has been telling me everything about you," he replied impishly then looked over at Debbie and gave her a wink.

"Debbie, you haven't!"

"Of course not," she retorted.

"Oh good," she said somewhat relieved.

"Or did I?" she said teasingly and winked back at Michael.

"You two are as bad as one another," she declared shaking her head. "I have to go or I'm going to be late."

"I have to get going, too, Mom and Dad are expecting me home for dinner," she explained turning to Michael. "It was lovely meeting you."

"You, too, Debbie," said Michael.

Debbie put on her coat and stood next to Emily.

"I should be home around eleven," confirmed Emily. "Ava, come say goodbye."

Ava came downstairs, kissed them both, and said bye. Then they said goodbye to Michael and left.

Debbie waited till they were far enough down the driveway. "Emily, he is adorable, charming, and handsome. What are doing with Brad?"

"Brad has some good qualities too."

"Like what?" she asked in disbelief.

"He's kind and generous."

"If you call throwing money around as being kind and generous, then you have no arguments here."

Emily was getting a little upset with her younger sister. "What are you trying to say, Deb?"

She looked at her Emily fondly. "You already know, Em. Michael is a good man, Ava adores him, and I think you do too. I just want you to make the right choices and be happy that's all."

"You're always looking out for me," said Emily, touched by her sister's concern.

"Always," replied Debbie. "I love you, Em."

"Love you, Deb."

Debbie put her arms around Emily whispering, "follow your heart."

"I will," she whispered back.

They said goodbye. Debbie left for home while Emily drove to work. On the way Emily thought about what her sister had said, 'follow your heart.'

Emily got home after midnight and noticed Michael was asleep on the couch. She quietly crept around the room, turned off the television, and covered him with a blanket. Then went into the kitchen, poured a glass of water, and stood in the doorway watching him sleep. She wanted to lie next to him and have him hold her, but with him being in such a deep sleep and Ava upstairs, she was afraid they would sleep through the night only to be woken by her in the morning. Instead, she put the empty glass in the sink, turned off the kitchen light, and went upstairs and got ready for bed. Emily regretted her decision as she tossed and turned till she fell asleep.

Chapter 26

"You were up and out early this morning," commented Emily as she sat next to Michael on the couch. "You were in such a deep sleep last night I thought Ava would be waking you up."

"I left around seven, luckily I had the alarm set on my phone, otherwise Ava would have been waking me up," he explained. "I guess I was tired from our night out and letting you win at pool."

"You did not!" she countered. "You're lucky I let you win that one game."

"I am, am I?" he asked doubtfully.

Emily made a sad expression. "I felt sorry for you."

"That's it!" said Michael trying to sound serious. "Next time we play pool, no more Mr. Nice Guy, you're going down."

"Oh, I'm so scared," she said laughing at him trying to be tough. "No more Mr. Nice Guy," she repeated humorously which made him laugh.

"I'm guessing next time we should put a bet on each game, so I can watch you crack under pressure," he said playfully.

Emily went serious. "Fine, as long as I can bring my own cue with me?"

"What? Really, you have one?" he asked, uncertain.

"Do you want to see it?" she went to stand.

"No," he said pulling her down, "that's okay, I believe you."

She burst out laughing. "You should have seen the look on your face."

"I'm going to get you for that, no more…Mr. Nice Guy," he said looking at her then the stairs. "I'll give you a five second head start."

"Oh no!" she yelled dramatically as she took off up the stairs.

Five seconds later he ran after her, hearing her bedroom door close, he went inside her room. Noticing the bathroom door was closed he walked over to it. "Here I come," he taunted, and slowly opened it, but couldn't see her. She must be hiding behind the shower curtain, he thought. Pulling it to one side he screamed, "A-ha!" she wasn't there.

"A-ha!" said a voice from behind him as she closed the bathroom door, ran out the bedroom, and down the stairs. She grabbed a blanket, jumped onto the couch, threw it over herself, and lay motionless.

Michael walked down the stairs slowly and quietly and moved towards her. "I got you now," he said tickling her till she begged him to stop. He removed the blanket from her face, her hair was covering part of it, so he moved it out of the way. She looked beautiful and he wanted to kiss her. Suddenly, the front door handle was moving, they both jumped, and sat up.

"Hi, Ava, how was your afterschool playdate?" asked her mom, straightening herself out.

"It was amazing," she replied looking at her mom with a funny face.

"What's wrong?"

"What's with your hair?" she asked. "It's all messy."

Michael looked over and laughed, so did Ava.

Emily looked in the mirror, turned around, and made a funny face at them. "I can't go to work looking like this!"

"You should Mom," suggested Ava laughing as she watched her leave.

When Emily came down, Michael was helping Ava make a Christmas card for Debbie, and when Ava noticed her, she ran over to whisper something in her ear then they both turned toward Michael.

"Ava wants to ask you something."

"Okay," replied Michael. "What?"

"On Wednesday evening we're having a Christmas Concert at school, and I was wondering if you would like to come and watch me?"

"I would love to," he replied with a smile, "thank you for asking."

"Yay," she screamed as she ran over to hug him.

"I have a surprise for you," he said mysteriously.

"Tell me, tell me!" she said impatiently.

Michael laughed at her reaction it reminded him so much of Emily.

"Now you know where she gets it from," admitted Emily.

"I do," agreed Michael with a nod then gave his attention back to Ava. "On Friday the twenty-third, my niece and nephews are coming over to help decorate my house. We are also going to have pizza, candies, and a sleepover. Would you like to come?"

"I would love that!" she said. "Mom, can I go, please?"

"Of course, you can."

She ran over to her mom and gave her a big squeeze.

"I'll see you in the morning, bed by eight," she said kissing the top of her head. "I should be home around eleven," she confirmed to Michael. Then said goodbye to them both and left.

Chapter 27

Emily and Ava arrived at the school thirty minutes before the concert. Michael agreed to meet them there just before seven, so Emily saved him a seat next to hers, and was watching the door closely. She spotted him walking into the gymnasium, smiled, stood, and waved to get his attention. Emily's parents and Debbie looked at one another, then her.

"He's here," she said looking at her family then noticed they were all staring at her. "What?"

"You just seem very happy he is here, is all," whispered her mom.

"Mom, Ava really wanted him to be here," she replied in her defense, "she would have been so disappointed if he hadn't shown up."

"Only Ava would have been disappointed?" questioned her teasing sister.

Emily looked down the row at her. "You are so lucky Mom and Dad are between us," she said pretending to be upset with her and disapprovingly looking away, then turned back towards Debbie. "Okay, I would have been disappointed too," she said sticking her tongue out at her. Debbie was laughing but not looking at her, Emily turned around to look up at Michael, and slowly put her tongue back in her mouth. "You made it!" she said with a grin.

"Of course," he replied. "It's such a lovely evening, I decided to walk, and it took me a little longer than I expected," he explained. He looked past Emily, said hello to her family, and sat. "Should I ask about the tongue thing," he whispered.

She blushed. "Just me and Deb being sisters."

The concert started; one by one each of the classes from kindergarten up to grade eight came onto the stage and sang Christmas songs. When Ava's class came on, they were all wearing antlers, had red noses, and sang 'Rudolph the Red Nose Reindeer,' plus two others. After the last class performed, everyone was invited to stay for refreshments. They congratulated Ava when she joined them then watched her take off with her friends to get cookies and juice. The adults drank their coffees, talked about Ava's pretty dress, and the concert. Eventually they said goodnight, Emily's parents and Debbie drove home, while Emily drove Ava and Michael to their place. Inside, Ava stayed up for a few minutes looking at pictures and videos from her concert which her mom had taken then she put her to bed before joining Michael on the couch.

"You must be tired?" he asked watching her collapse next to him.

"Exhausted," she replied with a sigh.

"I should go and let you get some sleep."

"I wouldn't mind unwinding and watching a movie," she said looking at him. "Do you want to watch one with me?"

"Yeah, I would like that, "he replied, "I could do with a little unwinding myself."

They made hot chocolate, ate homemade cookies, and sat close together watching the movie. Before it finished, Emily had fallen asleep on his shoulder. Michael picked her up, carried her upstairs, and put her on the bed then covered her with the duvet. Downstairs he turned everything off, closed the door, and walked home.

Chapter 28

Emily closed the door, took off her coat, and kicked off her shoes. I'm glad that day is over, she thought, walking into the kitchen. "I'm sorry for falling asleep on you last night," she said apologetically.

"It's okay," he replied.

"Did you carry me to bed?" she asked shyly. "Or did you drag me up the stairs?"

"I carried you; it was a struggle after all those cookies you ate," he kidded. "It probably would have been easier dragging you."

"Why, you!" she said gently pushing him. "Thank you, it was wonderful waking up in bed."

"No problem," he replied. "So, daughter and Mom night, tonight?"

"Yes, I've been so busy these last few nights, I'm looking forward to spending time with her," she replied. "She wants to eat at McDonald's, run around the play area, followed by Christmas cartoons here."

"It will be good for the both of you, you both need it," he suggested. "Do you want me to sit with her while you get ready?"

"That would be great," she said and headed for the stairs. Fifteen minutes later she walked into the living room, casually dressed in jeans with her hair in a ponytail. "I don't have to be too fancy for a Big Mac and fries," she replied a little self-conscious.

"You look very pretty," said Michael complimenting her as he put on his coat.

"Thank you," she said, blushing "Oh, I almost forgot." She grabbed a folder from the table. "My dad dropped these off on Wednesday, before the concert, they're my short stories."

"Great," he said keenly flipping through the folder, "I can't wait to read them."

"I hope you like them?" she asked nervously.

"I'm sure I will."

"I'll see you tomorrow," she said walking with him to the door.

He was about to reply when there was a knock on it, Emily opened it.

"Hey, Emily, miss me," said Brad sauntering in.

"Brad!" said Emily surprised.

"It's Thursday, I'm back," he said, noticing her confused look. "Remember dinner, tonight?" He glanced over at Michael. "Are you heading home?" he asked, not even waiting for a reply then looked at the table. "Where are the roses I gave you?"

Emily's face went red; she didn't dare make eye contact with Michael. "I…I put them upstairs in my bedroom."

"So, you get to see them when you first wake up, and before you go to sleep, good call," he said confidently. "Did you get a chance to read through the college material I left you? Maybe fill out the registration?"

"No, I've been too busy," she responded devastated. Now she definitely didn't want to look at Michael, but she needed to see his reaction, he was glaring at her.

"Well, no rush," continued Brad.

She looked away from Michael at Brad. "No, no rush," she replied quietly.

Michael put on a smile "I should get going let you guys enjoy your dinner and night."

Brad moved out of the way, opened the door, and patted him on the back. "Will do sport, you too, goodnight."

"Goodnight, Michael," said Emily, "I'll see you tomorrow." Not sure now if he would show.

"Goodnight, Emily," he replied leaving without making eye contact with her.

Her heart sank; she wanted to follow him outside and explain everything but decided it wasn't the right time. The sound of Brad loudly closing the door interrupted her thoughts.

"Let's get some dinner," he said as he turned toward her. "Where's the Munchkin?"

"Hold on one second!" she said grabbing his arm. "What are you doing here?"

He looked confused. "I said I would be back today, Thursday, we said we would go for dinner."

"You didn't text me to see if it was still okay or not," she said upset. "I have plans with Ava tonight."

"Oh, I didn't realize," he said trying to sound regretful.

She was quiet.

Brad stared at her. "Emily when I left, we agreed we would go for dinner tonight. You've been busy, I've been busy, I just wanted to see you," he explained as the salesman in him took over. "I drove straight here from the airport to be with you, if you want me to drive all the way home, and eat alone…I understand," he pitched starting for the door.

She felt bad for him. "We're going to McDonald's, you can come with us, but you have to leave when we get home. I'm spending the evening with Ava."

His pitch was sold, bought, and the deal was sealed. "Deal…I mean not a problem," said Brad. He hadn't had McDonald's in years and wasn't looking forward to it. "We could go somewhere fancier," he hinted.

"Brad!" snapped Emily.

As any good salesman knows, always know when to quit, and fix any lingering damage. "Now that I think about it, McDonald's will be fine. I haven't had it in years, it'll be fun," he lied.

They ordered their food, ate, and watched Ava run off to the play area.

"How was your trip?" she asked distantly.

"Excellent, we signed a huge deal! I should be looking at a big commission," he bragged, waiting for it to sink in.

"Good for you I'm sure you deserve it," she said, wondering how big it was.

"How's work going?" he asked, starting his second pitch.

"It's going well, I've received a lot more shifts, and hopefully I will get a few more. It's—"

"Can I ask you something?"

"Sure," she replied, a little annoyed she had been cut off.

"In January, won't you have to work as many hours as you are now?"

"Not necessarily, right now I am catching up on the couple months I'm behind," she clarified.

"But you will have to work more hours?"

"You mean to stay ahead?" she said and thought more about what he had asked.

"Yeah, to stay afloat, so you don't sink again," he said choosing his words very carefully, but to the point.

"I guess," she replied, having never really thought of it that way.

"Isn't Michael only helping you out till the end of the month? I mean, you can't be expecting him to keep on babysitting for you in January?" he said and could see her mind turning at his questions.

"We've never talked about January," she said unsure, "we only talked about December."

"Oh, maybe he can!" he suggested craftlly. "I'm sure if you ask him, he won't mind putting off his writing to babysit for you." Brad was on a role.

"No, I wouldn't…I couldn't do that to him," she replied quietly.

"If he doesn't, wouldn't you have to work even more hours to pay for a babysitter?"

"I would," Emily answered, Brad was making sense.

He took a few sips of his coffee to let her think a little longer about what he had said. "What's Michael's plan next year?"

She told him.

"He's committed to his writing then," he stated, "and his money is just to support him, and his writing."

"Seems that way," she said agreeing with him.

"So, he's not in the position to help out anyone financially," he concluded, letting it hang out there for a moment, then he went for the jugular. "And if he doesn't publish any books by next year, he will be broke, probably have to move back with his parents and look for a job."

"Probably," she said, becoming very, uncomfortable.

Brad paused for a moment, then did something very clever, he looked for Ava and got her attention. He waved and she waved back. "Look Ava's waiving."

Emily turned and waved to her.

He waited for Ava to continue playing which would force Emily to turn and face him. "You know Ava's a great kid, she deserves a chance at a good life, a comfortable life, one in which her mother is around all the time."

"I know, she does," replied Emily, Ava was Emily's life.

"And so do you Emily, so do you," he said reaching over, squeezing her hand, and making eye contact. "The best decision is an informed one. Read through the college material and think about what we talked about here tonight. Once you have all the information, you can then make that informed decision," advised Brad, and then came the sentimental angle. "Emily, you and Ava are the priority in my life, and it's important for me that you two have a good and happy one, I can give you that good and happy life." His pitch was sold.

"I know," she said quietly. She didn't want to talk or think about it anymore tonight. "It's late we should get going," she said, calling Ava over and putting on their coats.

Brad dropped them off at home. Emily and Ava went inside, put on their pajamas, snuggled, and watched cartoons.

Chapter 29

Emily nervously waited for Michael to arrive. She had texted him to see if he could come a little earlier, so they could talk, which he had agreed to. She was on her way down the stairs when she heard him come in and call out her name.

"How are you doing?" she asked.

"I'm doing well," he replied, "I've been busy running doing personal errands, and picking up groceries." He noticed she didn't look herself. "How are you?"

"I'm a little worried," she said trying to keep it together. "I'm sure you have questions for me, about Brad, about last night?"

When Michael left her yesterday, he was angry, and on the way here, he was still upset. But seeing her now, he wasn't either of those, he felt sorry for her. Michael moved towards her, held her in his arms, and told her, "everything's going to be okay."

She started to cry.

"Hey, hey, there's no need for tears," he said waiting till she stopped. "Come, sit with me, and we'll talk about it."

Emily followed Michael and sat next to him on the couch. "I want you to know what happened yesterday wasn't planned. Ava and I were supposed to be going for a girls' night out. Brad wasn't invited and I wasn't lying to you."

"I know, I know," he replied comforting her. "Why don't you tell me the whole story, start from the very beginning?"

She told him about the day Brad showed up with the roses and college information.

"Why didn't you tell me about the roses?"

"I was actually going to throw them out, instead, I put them in my room so you or Ava wouldn't see them."

"Why?"

"I don't know?" she replied. "The day before he had said something out of line, he apologized straight away, but I didn't believe him. I think the roses were supposed to be part of his apology, although he never actually said so, and because I didn't believe him, I didn't want them," she explained. "I also found them excessive and inappropriate. He does things like that on purpose to show off. And of course, he has to mention them in front of you. This made me realize that his bragging about them and rubbing them in your face was more important than the reason he had given them to me in the first place. I wish I had just tossed them out."

"I understand," he replied and thought for a moment. "I was in you room I never saw them."

"I knew you were coming in, so I hid them in the closet and ended up leaving them there," she explained. "I threw them out today."

"What about the college information?"

"In his own way, I guess he is trying to be encouraging, and show me what they offer. I meant to look through it, but I've been so busy," she said. "But once again, he has to blurt it out in front of you and put me on the spot."

"Emily, what he gives you, what you do with it, and what you talk about with him is your business, not mine. We've always maintained we're just friends. I will always leave it up to your discretion as to what you want to tell me," explained Michael, pausing. "But you're right, when he talks so openly in front of me, it makes me feel like you're hiding things from me and that, makes me feel like you're not being honest."

"I know I'm sorry, I should have talked to you about everything, I was wrong."

He smiled at her. "No harm done."

"Thank you," she replied, hugging him. As she held him, she decided not to discuss what she and Brad had talked about at McDonalds, that was for another day. She needed to get past this first. Besides, she needed more time to think about what Brad had said, and was actually glad she was going to work, it would distract her mind for a while.

Work wasn't busy and she was home by ten. Michael was sitting reading a magazine when she sat next to him.

"You're home early," he said placing it on the coffee table.

"It was a slow night," she replied.

"I should get going," he said standing up.

"Don't you want to hang around for a while?"

"No, I'm kind of tired, and I wouldn't mind an early night," he said putting on his jacket.

"All right," she replied a little surprised. She wanted to ask if everything was okay but decided not to. "I'll see you tomorrow morning, around ten?"

"Ten," he repeated, "goodnight," and walked out the door.

Emily stood by the door for a while thinking about what had just happened.

Chapter 30

"Did you get my text?"

"Yeah, you said your sister will be here around two," confirmed Michael.

"Okay, I wasn't sure if you received it, you didn't reply," she stated wondering why.

"I slept in and was running late," he said truthfully. "I just read it on my way here."

"As long as you received it," she said believing him.

"On the subject of texts, can I ask you something?"

"Sure, come into the kitchen, I just made coffee."

He sat at the table, Emily handed him a coffee, and sat next to him.

"What's on your mind?"

"You don't have to answer this if you don't want to," he said cautiously.

"You can ask me anything," she established wondering what it was.

"When Brad is away, do you text each other a lot?"

"No, not really, he tends to text me about what he is doing," she replied. "Like, I'm going into a big meeting, out for dinner with clients, back at the hotel. Mostly work related."

"Mostly?"

She wasn't too sure where he was going with this. "Sometimes he will ask me general stuff. Usually, if everything is okay and I just reply yeah, but they are few and far between."

Michael went quiet.

"Why do you ask?" she asked.

"It's nothing, I was wondering if you did, that's all" he replied. "I never see you text him and you never say that you have to."

"Trust me, ninety-nine percent of the time it's about his work. Last week when he was away, he texted me five times, tops!"

"I just wanted you to know that you can text him while I'm with you and you don't have to hide the fact that you text one another," he explained. That was partially true, but since yesterday's fiasco it had been bothering him how often they did text, and to a greater degree the contents of those texts and if they were intimate. He also wondered how they were when they were together, alone.

Emily suddenly realized Michael wasn't just interested in how often they text. "Do you want to know if we send intimate texts to one another?"

Michael went silent again.

"Well, we don't," she said bluntly.

"That's none of my business," he replied.

"You already know what he is like with me, you have seen us together, and you've probably already figured out he isn't the type to send me intimate texts either," as she said this, she realized something didn't seem right.

Emily was right, in seeing the two of them in front of him, he would have guessed that he wasn't that way. "In my defense, I am not with you and Brad when you two are alone, and I don't know how he acts with you or you with him." he replied. Just like Brad doesn't know what we are like when he's not around.

"You don't have to worry about that," she replied, "I'm not hiding anything there." Something about this conversation was troubling, something was bothering Michael, and she needed to know what. She was just about to ask him when.

"You're going to be late for work," said Michael.

Looking at the clock she realized he was right and decided to pick up the conversation with him another time. She jumped up, got ready, and came downstairs. "Ava will be home from her playdate in thirty minutes. Debbie will be here at two. She is staying over tonight and sticking around till I finish work tomorrow."

"Okay," replied Michael quietly.

"Looks like you will have lots of free time this afternoon, and tomorrow, bet you're looking forward to it?" she asked jokingly.

"I am," he replied, "I'm tired, and I could do with the break."

Emily was hurt by his response, but just said, "goodbye," and quickly left. As she walked down the driveway to her car, she stopped twice, each time thinking about going back in to ask him what he meant by, 'I could do with a break.' Since she didn't want to be late for work, she decided to ask him next time she saw him.

Ava was home from her playdate at eleven; they made a snowman in the backyard, and then went inside to have lunch. As they ate, they talked about it being seven days till Christmas Eve, about Santa, and about presents. At two Debbie showed up. Ava hugged Michael, said goodbye, and he left.

Emily received a text from Debbie saying she had arrived, then another saying she was going to take Ava to the movies and would be home around nine. She was almost finished her shift when Brad walked in.

"How's your day been?" he asked.

"Steady," she replied.

"Is Michael watching Ava?"

"Well, he was till two, and then my sister came over and is taking Ava to the movies and staying the night." She couldn't stop the words coming out about the movies.

"Then you have a free night," he said favorably.

"No, not really, I need to be home before they are. I promised Deb I would hang out with her." Which wasn't the truth, but it was what she wanted to do.

"What are you doing for dinner?"

"I'm going to eat at home," she replied. "I'm tired."

"You've been working all day, let me take you out for a well-deserved meal," he said, not really asking, "and let someone else cook for you."

"I don't know, by the time I go home, and get ready." She wasn't in the mood.

"The place I have in mind is casual, close, and we can leave straight from here. I promise to have you home before your sister," negotiated Brad.

"Okay," she said succumbing to him "I'll meet you at your car in ten minutes." Emily finished up, got in his car, and they drove to a steakhouse. As they ate their meals and drank their wine, Emily started to listen to Brad talk about work, but her mind drifted as she thought about last Saturday night playing pool and dancing with Michael. She wondered what he was doing tonight, and if he was thinking about their night out, and about her. She thought about their conversation this morning, something was bothering him, and she needed to talk to him about that. Then she thought about what Brad had said about Michael, about going to college, and moving to the city, about Aurora, editing in the new year, and Michael helping her. About Ava, work, her finances, and what Debbie had said about 'following your heart.' She couldn't stop thinking about everything! Her head was spinning. Emily wondered why her life had become so complicated and confusing these last few days.

"…and that's how we finalized the deal," said Brad finishing his story.

"That's great," replied Emily, with no clue as to what he had just said.

"Did you give any more thought to what we talked about the other day?" he asked testing the waters.

"Can we not talk about that tonight?" she pleaded.

Understanding it was not in his best interests to pursue this discussion, he changed his tactics. "No rush, you go ahead and take your time, and think it all through."

Michael spent the remainder of the afternoon at home. Dropped by his parents for an hour to help his dad move some furniture, and then went out for the night with Kristen, Joshua, and several other friends he hadn't seen for a while. As he drank, he thought about last Saturday night playing pool and dancing with Emily, and smiled to himself as he recalled the night. He then reflected on the last couple of days, and Emily being with Brad, and his smile disappeared. He tried not to think about her, but it was difficult, feelings aside, Emily was his friend, and he knew what he had to do.

As Brad had promised Emily was home before Ava and Debbie. She changed, went into the kitchen, and poured herself a long glass of wine. She heard the front door open, the sound of Ava running towards her and listened as she told her about the movie her and Debbie had seen.

"I'm glad to hear you enjoyed it," said Emily as she gave her a kiss. "Now upstairs, quickly, pajamas."

"I can do with one of those, "suggested Debbie looking at Emily's wine.

"Coming right up!" she said pouring a glass and handing it to her,

"Is everything okay with Michael?" asked Debbie as they walked into the living room.

"Why do you ask?"

"He didn't seem like himself today. He seemed quiet and preoccupied."

"I'm not sure," replied Emily although she knew something was bothering him. "Did Ava mention anything?"

"I asked her at the movies how he was, she just said, 'the same old Michael, fun, fun, fun,' her words, not mine," clarified Debbie. "Ava said they made a snowman today then had a soup and sandwich for lunch." Debbie looked over at Emily. "She reveres him."

"I know she does," agreed Emily, "she really has taken a shine to him."

"Where is he tonight?"

"I'm not sure," she replied wondering that same question herself.

"Oh, okay," said Debbie deciding it was best to let it go.

"Did you two eat?"

"We ordered pizza before we left, there is some in the fridge if you're hungry?"

"No, I'm good, I went out for dinner with Brad," she said unenthusiastically.

"With Brad?" repeated Debbie a little surprised.

"He came to my work. It wasn't planned."

"Wow Emily! You really sound happy and excited about your dinner date with your boyfriend!" she said sarcastically.

"I really wasn't in the mood to go," she said quietly, "I have a lot of things on my mind."

"I'm sorry," said Debbie putting her arm around her sister. Emily rested her head on Debbie's shoulder, closed her eyes, and thought.

Chapter 31

Emily woke up, went downstairs, gave Ava a bowl of cereal, and made a pot of coffee. Shortly after, Debbie joined her, poured a coffee, and sat at the kitchen table next to her.

"How did you sleep?" asked Debbie.

"I tossed and turned all night."

"You look tired."

"I need an early night," she said yawning, "I think that will be tonight, in bed by nine."

"It will do you the world of good," said Debbie, thinking as she looked over her sister's shoulder at Ava eating her cereal and watching television. Debbie leaned towards Emily and whispered. "Is there anything you want to talk about?"

"I don't know," Emily replied, "yes and no," as she put her hands to her head then through her hair. "I think I'm working so much it's getting me down. I'm not around as much as I should be for Ava, and I feel like I have no free time."

"It's only for the holidays, once you get caught up, you can work less," said Debbie trying to comfort her.

"I'm worried come January, I will have to do it all over again," she confessed.

"Take it one month at a time. Worry about this month now and next month later," she said supportively. Debbie could tell there was more to it than that. "There's something else, what is it?"

Emily smiled at her; her sister knew her too well. "As you know, Michael has been such a great help, but I can't expect him to keep on doing this next month, and the month after that, it's not fair. He has his own life to live, and he has his writing."

"Have you talked to him about it?"

"No."

"Don't you think you should?

"No."

"No?" questioned Debbie. "It seems like you are speaking on his behalf and not giving him the benefit of the doubt. He needs a chance to speak for himself, and I think you need to give him that opportunity."

"I don't know," said Emily miserably, "something is wrong with him, and I'm not sure what it is."

"What do you mean?"

"Yesterday morning before I left, I joked he would have a lot of free time on his hands after you arrived." She gave her sister a sad look. "He said he was tired and could use the break."

"And?"

"What do you mean, and?" she replied with her back up.

"You just said the exact same thing to me, you're tired, you want some free time, an early night," reminded Debbie and waited for her response. Instead, Emily's eyes started to water, and then it dawned on her. "Oh, you think he means he needs a break from you."

She nodded her head as she held back the tears. "He's been acting differently toward me these last couple of days: I know it, I can feel it, and I can see it. You even said he wasn't himself."

"Emily what happened? Something else has happened since Wednesday. Tell me!" she said in a stern voice.

"What do you mean?"

"Wednesday at the concert you were so happy to see him, and he was too. You guys were glowing and smitten. All the way home, Mom, Dad, and I talked about you two, how good you looked together," said Debbie. "I like him, Mom and Dad like him, what happened?"

She told her about Brad giving her the roses and the college information. The Thursday night when Brad showed up with Michael standing by the door. Her conversations with Michael Friday evening and yesterday morning, and the way Michael has been acting. Emily left out the conversation with Brad at McDonald's.

"Oh boy!" said Debbie sitting back.

"Friday afternoon before I went to work, we talked about what happened with Brad on Thursday evening, and he said there was no harm done and we hugged. I thought we got passed it. But the way he acted when I got home Friday night and on Saturday morning, I don't believe him," she said upset. "For him to be saying no harm done and then to act that way is wrong, and I think Michael is being unfair!"

Debbie gave Emily a look she had never seen before.

"What?" asked Emily.

Debbie let her have it. "You have some nerve saying that Emily, after what Michael has done for you. Babysitting your daughter, picking her up from the bus stop, helping her with her homework, making pizza, cookies, snowman, and putting her to bed. He has made you dinner, stayed around after you finish work to keep you company, and waited late nights for you to come home. He even leaves before Ava wakes up. It was Michael that went to Ava's concert, helped you cut down your tree, decorate it, and you're living room…and they're the only the things I can remember off the top of my head," she said. "And why? Why did he do this? So that you could work extra hours to pay off your bills, get caught up, and maybe get ahead…In summation, to help you out!" Debbie stopped for a moment to calm down. "Has he ever asked you for anything in return? And don't you dare bring up editing his manuscript! Has he? Has he?"

"No," she said in a low voice, ashamed of what she had said about him.

"No, is right. Yet you let Brad waltz in here, spout off his mouth, and cause ripples," continued Debbie. "When has Brad ever helped you or Ava out? Ava never mentions his name! He doesn't spend any time with her!"

"It's because he doesn't want to get too attached to her, in case we stop seeing one another," she said in his defense.

"You are actually defending him," she said angrily. Then Debbie spurted out something she wished she hadn't. "You and Brad are the same, all you care about are yourselves, then criticize those around you that care about you Emily. No wonder Michael wants a break from you, who wouldn't, you sound like a spoilt brat!" Debbie felt awful. "Emily, I'm sorry I didn't mean that."

Emily burst into tears and took off up the stairs. She threw herself on the bed, put her face in the pillow, and continued to cry.

Debbie went after her, sat on the edge of the bed, and gently stroked her sister's back. "Emily, I'm so sorry, I didn't mean that last bit, please forgive me."

Emily moved over, put her head on her sister's lap, sobbing. "I'm so confused."

"I know," said Debbie comforting her, "I know."

Emily eventually stopped crying and sat up. "I need to shower and get ready for work."

"Em, I'm sorry about the last part, I really didn't mean it."

"I know," she said stroking Debbie's sad face. "What you said was true, and sometimes the truth isn't always easy to hear. Thank you, you're a great sister."

Debbie smiled, gave Emily a hug, and left.

Thirty minutes later she came downstairs, said bye, and left.

Michael lay in bed wondering what to do today. He was so used to getting ready to go to Emily's, he was at a loss. He eventually got up, ate breakfast, and decided to go for a walk. He stopped in at the coffee shop, sat there for a while, and watched people come and go. Once he'd finished, he continued his walk and ended up at his parents' place and dropped in to have a talk with them.

Work was slow, making the day drag, and giving Emily too much time to think about things she would rather not. Five o'clock finally came, she went home and made dinner with Ava and Debbie, and then ate.

During which Debbie talked about their shopping trip while Ava showed off her new dress. After Debbie left, Emily watched a movie with Ava then put then put her to bed. At nine, Emily slid under the sheets, and tossed and turned all night.

After dinner, Michael slowly walked home from his parents. All day he tried to get Emily out of his mind, but no matter how hard he tried, he couldn't. As he took off his coat, he noticed the folder on the dining room table; it was Emily's short stories. He counted twelve in total. Michael lay on his bed and started to read them. After finishing the fifth he looked over at the time, almost eleven, he closed the folder and placed it on his dresser. He got ready for bed, crept under the sheets, and tried desperately to fall asleep.

Chapter 32

Present Day – Monday, December 19

The school bus pulled to a stop and the children disembarked one by one. Ava was second to last, noticing Michael, she screamed his name and jumped into his arms.

"I missed you this weekend. Where have you been?"

"I missed you, too," he said twirling her around before putting her down. "Well, your aunt Debbie wanted some time with you, which gave me some free time, to do some things that I needed to do."

"Okay," she said as she held his hand and merrily skipped home.

Michael helped her take off her coat before going into the kitchen and making hot chocolate.

"Here are the marshmallows," said Ava placing them on the kitchen table then grabbed a handful and placed them in her mug.

"Can you put some in mine?" asked Michael.

"Will do," she said cheerfully.

"What did you do with your aunt Debbie Saturday?"

Ava told her about playing games, ordering pizza, going to the movie, and watching television with her and her mom.

"You had a lot of fun, then?"

"So much fun!" she said excitedly as she sipped her hot chocolate. "Yesterday, we went shopping, had lunch, then we made dinner with Mom."

"Wow!" exclaimed Michael.

"And Aunt Debbie bought me a new dress," she said taking off, coming back, and showing him.

"That is beautiful!"

"It's so pretty. I'm going to wear it Christmas Eve."

"Which is only five days away!" said Michael in an excited voice.

"I know I can't wait!"

They did some coloring, made dinner, and watched television. Ava went to bed, and around ten, Emily walked in, tired and irritable.

"How was Ava?"

"As good as gold," replied Michael managing a smile and standing up to leave.

"Are you leaving, again?" she asked sharply.

"Yeah," he said, surprised by her tone.

Emily let out a long sigh. "Can we talk, please?"

"Sure," replied Michael taking a seat.

"What's wrong?" she asked sitting next to him. "You've been avoiding me like the plague, you take off as soon as I get home, and you hardly say two words to me."

"I'm confused about us," he said candidly. "I just think we need some space."

"Space? As in taking a break, space?" she asked looking for more details.

"I just think we both need to take a step back and reevaluate what we are doing," he said honestly. "We say we're friends, but we've crossed that line on several occasions, and it's not right with you seeing Brad."

"Oh, this is about Brad!" she snapped, her tiredness and irritability getting the better of her.

"I didn't say that," corrected Michael, "this is about you and me. Brad is your concern, not mine."

"My concern, in what way?"

"Well, isn't he your boyfriend?"

"We go on dates."

He gave her an odd look. "Do you date anyone else?"

"No."

"To me, that makes him your boyfriend, and you a couple."

"Okay, just to keep this moving along, he's my boyfriend, and we're a couple, and?" she asked impatiently.

He thought for a moment. "Let me try to explain this in the simplest way."

"Oh, because I'm simple!" she said mockingly.

Michael took a deep breath, ignored her response, and continued. "Do you tell Brad everything we do?"

"No, not everything."

"Not everything or none of it?"

"Not everything." In truth Brad knew very little.

"Why not?"

Emily felt like she was being pushed into a corner and didn't want to be trapped there. "Because…" she said hesitantly, not wanting to answer.

"Because…some of the things we do as friends he wouldn't approve of?" suggested Michael.

"I guess."

"Then that's a problem," established Michael. "If we only did what all other friends do, you should be able to tell him everything, right?"

Emily sighed heavily.

"Like I said earlier, we need to take a step back, take a break, and reevaluate."

She knew he was right about stepping over the friendship line and with Brad not knowing. "So, what about us?"

"Us?" he asked confused. "From day one you told me we were friends; we have reminded each other daily we are friends, and you even tell your family and your friends, that we are friends."

"I know what I tell them!" she said sharply.

"Emily, I am your friend, and you have a boyfriend, I shouldn't be holding you in your bed; it has to stop. And you know yourself; that's just one example of us crossing the line, we need to reset our boundaries," explained Michael calmly, "especially if we are going to continue to be just friends." Although deep down in his heart that wasn't what he wanted at all, or the way he truly felt about her.

Emily had been hoping to hear something completely different from him, she had feelings for him, and she thought he did for her. But what he was saying now was the total opposite, and it hurt her, and she wanted to hurt him back. "At least Brad can provide for Ava and me. He can afford to pay for my college, put Ava in a private school, and give us a very comfortable life," she retaliated furiously.

"And, what's your point?" asked Michael, wanting to hear her say it.

"He has a plan. What's your plan, Michael? To continue to write books, hoping one day you may get lucky, and maybe one day get one published. And if not, then what? Move back in with mommy and daddy when your money runs out," she said nastily.

"Money? Is that what's most important in your life, money!" he snapped back. "Is that the answer to all your problems?"

"It's better than working my butt off in a job I don't like, and having a child I don't see at nights," she countered.

"What about doing your editing in January?"

"Who is going to want me to edit their book?" she asked in dismay. "Someone like you, Michael, who can't afford to pay me! Even if your book gets published, who would even know I edited it? No one!"

"Emily, you've changed these last few days," said Michael shaking his head. "Did someone say something to you to make you feel like this? This is not the person I know; this is not who you are."

"Maybe someone opened my eyes to what you can't offer me," she said smirking smugly at him. "Besides, who wants to be with a penniless—" Emily stopped herself, she couldn't believe how far she had taken it.

"Say it," whispered Michael.

"No."

"Say it!" he said looking at her.

"No, I don't want to," she pleaded.

"Say it!" he demanded.

"Please, please stop…I don't want to say it."

"Well, let me say it for you…Penniless writer!" said Michael, distraught and extremely hurt. He looked away from her, slowly took a deep breath, and thought momentarily. He looked at her and took his time with what he had to say next. "Emily, you're right. I can't pay for you to go to college, put Ava in a private school, buy you a condo in the city, or give you a comfortable life. So, I will agree with you there, and say that you're one hundred percent right."

Emily saw the hurt in his eyes and had to look away.

"But what I can offer you is someone who you can talk to about anything, who will listen to you, and will genuinely care about what you have to say...someone who will be honest, sincere, caring, and kind…but most of all, someone who will give you love and support. Because the backbone to any couple, to us being friends, is the unconditional love and support you give to one another in good times, and more importantly, in bad times…Then again, maybe he already has all those things covered, you are a couple and I'm not around when you two are together, so I'm guessing he probably does…Which means it just comes down to you and Ava having a comfortable life." Michael hesitated and looked at her, judging by her silence, he was right. "Emily, I believed in you from the first day we met. The problem is you never believed in yourself…in me…and now in us," he said sadly, then stood, put on his coat, and headed for the door.

Emily realized replying was pointless, the damage had been done and whatever she said he wouldn't believe it anyway, and who could blame him. Instead, she remained silent and let him walk away from her. And as her eyes welled up, she wondered, "What she was doing?"

Michael glanced over at her one last time "Enjoy your money, your comfortable life…I'm sure Brad will be a great husband, a wonderful stepfather, and I wish you all the best, Emily." Then turned around, opened the door, and quietly closed it behind him.

Emily fell to the floor crying. Ten minutes later she pulled herself up, went upstairs, and skulked into bed. She thought about her conversation with Michael, it hadn't gone the way she had expected it to, and now she wasn't sure how to fix it. She wondered what had happened and how everything had gone so wrong so fast. Debbie was right, something had happened, but what? Emily thought back to the first time she met Michael, and then chronologically recalled the next event, then the next one, the next, and the next, and as she did, she recalled all their conversations. The more she ran them through her head, the more she began to notice something, a pattern. All of a sudden it hit her. She sat up in bed and said one word. Emily now knew what she had to do.

Chapter 33

The following morning Emily called in sick to work. She sent a text to Michael telling him she was home ill and didn't need him to babysit today, to which he only replied okay. She then sent one to Brad informing him she had something important to tell him and asked him to meet at her place at one o'clock, which he confirmed. Emily needed to think about what she was going to say to him and how she was going to say it. She decided a long walk may help and it did. When she returned, she ate lunch, and patiently waited for Brad. At one, there was a knock on the door.

"Come in Brad."

"Hello, Emily," he replied, "your text sounded urgent."

"It is," she confirmed, "have a seat."

"I'm hoping it's good news about you moving," he said with an air of confidence.

"Before we get to me moving to the city, I need to clear some things up with you first."

"Okay," he replied feeling more relaxed with her mentioning the words moving and city.

She took a breath and began. "That night I met Michael at the bar. When he walked me home, and I said I would edit his book, there were two things I realized about him. The first, I will get to later. The second, I will tell you now. When he accepted my offer to edit his manuscript, he took a leap of faith with me, do you know why?"

Brad shook his head.

"Because he could have had Robert Johnson edit it instead of me," she said looking at Brad. "Do you know who Robert Johnson is?"

"The famous journalist," he answered.

"Yes," she replied. "Michael had turned down the famous journalist Robert Johnson and picked me, a bartender with limited editing experience, over a journalist legend. He even had to go back to Robert Johnson to tell him his decision. Can you imagine the courage it would take to say no to one of the top journalists in the country and explain to him who you had picked instead?"

"That is something," replied Brad, "I didn't know he did that."

"Those weeks I spent editing his manuscript were the happiest I have been in a long time, I loved it so much, and I felt like the old me. It was like I had purpose in my life again, something to contribute and offer people, other than the special of the day!" The last bit she said in a comical way which made her giggle a little. "When I sat with Michael and reviewed my edits with him, he told me they were brilliant, excellent, amazing, and professional, and he kept every single one of my recommendations. Do you know how proud that made me feel? Do you know I told all my family and friends what I had accomplished? They were all so happy for me," she said and paused momentarily. "Michael said to me that in the new year I should consider editing. He suggested thinking about it, and if it was something I wanted to pursue, he would help me. Do you know why?"

"No," replied Brad.

"Because he said he believed in me," replied Emily and smiled as she remembered their conversation. "When he told me that, I really didn't know what he meant, and I took it as he believes that I will do a good job editing his manuscript. It wasn't till last night, I truly realized what he meant."

Last night, thought Brad, what happened last night?

"Michael believed in me so much he was willing to sacrifice it all for me. He entrusted his first manuscript to me, a bartender who hadn't even finished her degree, and he also believed in the new year, I could be an editor. Michael was so eager to help and support me that he asked nothing of me in return. At the time, when he said he believed in me, I didn't comprehend what it all encompassed, but now I do."

Brad was silent.

"As you are aware these last few weeks Michael has been taking care of Ava, not lying on the couch, and babysitting her, actually taking care of her. He helps with her homework, plays with her, cooks with her, puts her to bed, and so much more. He didn't have to do that, he really didn't" she said proudly. "He could have just sat around, put the television on and watched it with her, but he didn't. Do you know why he didn't?" asked Emily looking at Brad.

Brad didn't know the answer.

Not surprised he didn't, she looked away, and continued. "I guess I knew the answer all along, but I never really gave it too much thought until last night." She grinned at what she had come to realize. "The reason why Michael didn't just sit around, was because he wanted me to know that when I was at work, I could be confident knowing Ava was with a good person, and a person who genuinely liked her, and wanted to spend time with her. That he was someone who would take care of Ava's needs and who she would be happy with. Deep down, Michael wanted me to know that I had nothing to worry about. In me knowing this, it allowed me to work nights, longer shifts and double shifts without feeling any guilt, anxiety, or regret. And as well as taking care of Ava, he was also saving me money, and helping me make more money to get back on my feet. Michael sacrificed all his time for me, and never asked me once for anything in return," explained Emily, she paused for a moment thinking about how mean she had been to him last night, and how sorry she was. "During this time, he also befriended me, in fact he became my best friend, and I could talk to him about anything." Emily felt like she was going to cry, but contained herself, and carried on. "Michael said to me, and by the way this is the only similarity you two share, that when I make my decision, make sure it's an informed decision. The only difference is that he never pressured me, put me on the spot, made me feel awkward, or planted thoughts in my head. Last night—"

"Hold on Emily, you're being unfair!" contested Brad. "I never—"

"Let me finish Brad you…will have your chance to talk."

He went quiet.

She continued. "Last night Michael asked me if you knew everything about him and me. I replied not everything. The truth is, you know very little, but now I am going to tell you." Which she did, right down to kissing him on the cheek, cuddling him on the couch, and Michael holding her in bed. By Brad's expression she could tell he wasn't pleased at all, but she didn't care. "I kept on telling Michael that it was okay, this is what friends do, until last night he called me out on it. He told me that we had crossed the friendship line, that we needed to step back, and reevaluate. When he said that to me, I was extremely hurt, and I wanted to hurt him back, so I let him have it. Boy did I let him have it!" She stopped and glanced at Brad. "Do you remember the conversation you had with me in McDonald's, about Michael not being able to provide for me and Ava, and so on."

Brad nodded his head.

"I turned around and told him everything you said to me, almost to the word, except I didn't say it was you who said that…no, no, no, no," she said shaking her head. "I made him believe it was all coming from me, and that this is what I truly thought of him." She looked away from Brad and recalled the hurt in Michael's eyes. "But enough about Michael and me," she said. It was time for her to shift the conversation, and she looked at Brad and quietly said, "Brad, let's talk about you," then hesitated momentarily, "maybe you would prefer to talk first?"

With the way this conversation was heading Brad may have been many things, but he wasn't a fool. "No, go ahead," he replied, wanting Emily to play her hand first.

"Fair enough," she said with a smirk. "These last several weeks my life has been good, actually it has been amazing, and I've been extremely happy. I was editing, had someone taking care of Ava, was able to work more hours, and was getting back on my feet. Everything was fantastic. Then all of a sudden everything becomes complicated, and I'm burdened by these thoughts in my head. I'm confused, tired, and agitated at work and at home. And most importantly, Michael is starting to act strangely towards me, and avoiding me. So last night, I decided to confront him and ask him what was going on. He tells me. Instead of listening to him and talking it over like a friend, I unleashed my fury on him. I've not only insulted and chased away my best friend, but I have also denied Ava from having someone in her life who will take care of her like no other, and worse, someone whom she may never see again ever," said Emily sadly. "Last night, I'm lying in bed thinking to myself, what made me act the way I did? So, I start going through all the events and conversations leading up to last night, over, over and over again, in my mind. The more I ran through them, the more I began to notice something, a pattern. Then all of a sudden it hit me. It was right there in front of me the whole time. I finally had my answer. I sat up in bed and said one word." She looked into Brad's eyes. "Do you know what that word was?"

"No," he replied unsure.

"Brad!"

"Me?" he asked puzzled.

"Everything that has caused an issue in my life stems from you, from the day you put Michael down in your car right up to the conversation in McDonald's, it was all you," she revealed, pausing briefly. "But the two events that stand out most in my mind, is when you mentioned the roses and college information in front of Michael and me. The second, was your conversation at McDonald's. Both were brilliant. You knew by saying something about the roses and college in front of him, it would cause a ripple between us and that he would eventually ask me about them, resulting in tension between us. You also knew it would make Michael question my honesty, my integrity, our friendship, and maybe force him to back off. In return, I would get upset with him, maybe use that conversation you planted in my mind at McDonald's to get back at him, which as you now know, I did. You planned this all-out Brad, didn't you?"

"Do you hear yourself? Do you actually think I contrived this? You are making me sound like I'm—"

"Crazy," she suggested. "Brad you're not crazy, just an incredibly gifted salesman who I finally caught on to, maybe a little too late, but better late than never," said Emily steadfast. "You pitched, I almost bought it, but no deal."

For the first time in his life Brad was speechless.

She wasn't shocked by his reaction, so she continued. "At the beginning of our talk I said there were two things I realized the night I first met Michael, the second I have told you. The first is this, I'm in love with Michael, and I believe I fell in love with him the first night I met him."

Brad sat back letting out a deep sigh. "I know you are."

"You do?" she asked a little surprised.

Brad knew it was over, he realized if he cared about Emily, the least he could do was be completely honest with her and come clean. "That day I walked in through the entrance at your work, you were staring off in the distance, you had this glow on your face that I had never seen before. So, I turned to see what you were looking at, and it was Michael. That same day I asked you to walk me to the door, you did, and I hugged you unexpectedly. Do you remember?"

"I do."

"Out the corner of my eye I was looking to see if Michael was watching us, he was, so I hugged you. I thought it may shy him away," said Brad continuing his confession. "The night I picked you up at your house, and I went on about my Mercedes, I was trying to belittle him in front of you. Then later, when we were driving to the party, I called him a penniless writer, then apologized because—"

"Because after you call someone that and realize you were hurtful, you try to take it back by saying you meant it like you see in the movies, a penniless writer trying to publish their first big novel," said Emily. "It wasn't an apology at all, you wanted me to think it was, but it wasn't."

He laughed nervously. "Oh, you knew."

"I didn't know at that time, I found out later, by accident."

Brad realized Michael must have mentioned it to her. "When I took you out for the Italian dinner, you mentioned you were thinking about editing in the new year. I knew Michael had suggested that to you. I wanted to outdo him, so I upped the ante by suggesting you go to college."

"Why?" she asked.

"Please, let me tell you everything first, I'm on a role," he replied anxiously then collected his thoughts. "That Thursday when I showed up at your house, I knew he would be there, and you're right. I purposely mentioned the roses and the college information in front of him. I had a notion you hadn't told him, and by the look on his face, I knew you hadn't. I had a hunch it would cause tension between the two of you," he revealed and briefly paused. "In my defense, we did say we would go for dinner when I got back. The fact that you had planned a night with Ava, then me showing up, and going with you was only going to raise more questions in Michael's mind as to whether you had told him the truth or not. Being fairly confident you two would have words, I made my pitch in McDonald's regarding what I could offer you, and more importantly what he couldn't. I had my suspicion it would escalate between you two, and with my conversation at McDonald's being fresh in your mind, you may use it against him and end your relationship with him."

"Why?" she demanded. "Why would you do this to me?"

"You don't know?" he said disappointedly.

"No," she said honestly.

"I was losing you day by day," he replied, "and I was trying to fight for you in the only way I knew how, by showing you that my competitor was a liability."

"Competitor, liability," she repeated. "Why wouldn't you just be yourself and win me over that way?"

"That's the problem, I was being myself," he said sadly.

Emily felt sorry for him.

"The way Michael treats you, how he takes care of Ava, him freeing up your time so you can take extra shifts to catch up and believing in you and your editing; I couldn't compete with that." Brad shook his head and laughed a little. "He really is a wonderful guy and every suitor's worst nightmare," he said looking at Emily. "It's hard not to like him, I like him. If I were you, I would love him, too."

Emily giggled at what he said and reached out to hold his hand. "Brad you are a good man, too. You just need to meet someone who fits your lifestyle. Someone who is single, has no children, and will fly off anytime and anywhere with you at the drop off a hat. There were several girls at the party who fit that profile, some of them liked you, I could tell."

"Thank you," he said putting his free hand on top of hers. "I am so sorry for what I did."

"Thank you, Brad, you could have simply said I was crazy for what I was thinking and walked out the door. Instead, you were open with me, and confirmed what I thought was true, so that I could move on with my life," explained Emily, understanding it couldn't have been easy for him to come clean like he had.

"I hope you'll forgive me?" he asked genuinely.

"I do," she replied and hugged him.

"Michael is a very lucky man," he whispered, "and you are a very lucky woman."

"I know," she replied as she let go. "So, what's next for you then?"

Brad quickly changed back to being all business. "Well, I decided I am going to get the bigger condo for two reasons: one, as an investment; two, if I do meet someone down the road I won't have to move," he said with a chuckle. "This evening I'm going to meet with my real estate agent and have her put in an offer on a vacant condo. On Friday, I'm going to see my family for Christmas and hopefully before New Year's Eve, I can start moving into my new place."

"Looks like you have it all figured out," she said, happy for him.

"Pretty much," he replied then looked at the time. "I should get going," he said standing. "One more thing, is there anything I can do or say to Michael to help fix things between you two."

"No," she said appreciating his offer, "this is something I need to do on my own."

"I understand," he said putting on his coat.

"On Friday, try drop in and say bye before you leave," she suggested.

"I will," he said with a smile, and left.

As soon as the door closed Emily reached for her phone and called Michael's number. There was no answer and decided to leave a voicemail. "Hey, it's Emily, I know you are upset with me, and I don't blame you, but we need to talk. Please call me as soon as you get this message." She hung up, made a coffee, and sat, and waited, and waited, and waited. Emily sent him several texts over the next hour, still no response. She thought about going to his place but decided it wasn't a good idea and opted to wait for his reply instead. On the way to the bus stop, her phone beeped notifying her she had received a text, it was from Michael. Emily nervously read it.

Michael: "I received your texts, voicemail. I don't think it's a good time for us to talk now, maybe later."

Emily: "Please reconsider, I really need to talk to you."

Michael: "You said a lot of hurtful things."

Emily: "I know I did. Please meet me, please let me explain, please, please."

Michael: "I need some time, maybe in a few days."

She didn't want to wait a few days, she looked up and saw the school bus approaching, and had an idea. Emily texted him: "That's fine. Are you still okay to watch Ava tomorrow after school?" She anxiously waited for his response.

The school bus stopped, and Ava jumped off. "Mom!" she yelled joyfully running toward her. "Can we go to the store to get a card and present for my teacher?" she pleaded.

"Yes, we can," she replied.

"Yay!" she said as they walked home.

Ava dropped her bag in the hallway, and as Emily was reaching for her car keys, her phone beeped.

Michael: "Sorry for the delay I had to take a phone call. Of course, I'm okay to watch Ava and whenever else you need me to."

Emily: 'Thank you." She smiled to herself as she put her phone away. She would talk to Michael tomorrow, after she got home from work.

At the store Ava picked out a box of chocolates for her teacher then went to the card section. Emily spotted a card out of the corner of her eye and picked it up grinning. She wasn't sure if this was fate, destiny, or pure luck. She placed it in the basket with the chocolates then helped Ava pick one out. They paid for their items and went home.

After dinner Emily helped Ava write out the card, wrap her present, and put them into her school bag. Then Emily started to write out her card.

"Who is that for, Mom?" asked Ava looking on.

"This is Mommy's Christmas wish card," she said looking up at her.

"Are you going to put it under the tree next to mine?"

"Yes, I am," Emily replied, finishing it. She put it in the envelope then gave it to Ava to place under the tree.

"Mom, you forgot to put Santa's name on it." She reached for a red marker, wrote Santa on it and the date, December 20th, and then positioned it under the tree next to hers.

"Why did you put the date on it?" asked Emily curiously.

"That's so Santa knows how long you have been wishing for," she replied.

Chapter 34

Emily waved bye to Ava as the bus pulled away then she jumped into her car, drove to the coffee shop, and went inside. She stood by the front entrance looking around for Sue who was usually there before her. The door opened behind, Emily, who was so busy looking around, accidentally bumped into the girl coming in.

"I'm so sorry," said Emily looking at an incredibly attractive blonde.

"No worries," she said with a friendly smile, "no harm done."

Emily watched the blonde walk past around the partition and lift her arms out.

"Michael," she cried.

"Lauren."

Emily recognized his voice. She peeked through the glass partition to witness Michael hugging the blonde then kiss her on the cheek. Lauren, she thought, he did say Lauren. She wasn't one hundred percent that's what he called her, but judging by how cozy they were, it had to be his ex-girlfriend. Emily watched them sit across from one another, but with the noise of the people coming and going, she could barely make out what they were saying. But heard enough to confirm it was her; Emily's heart sank.

"Who are you spying on?" asked a voice from behind.

A startled Emily quickly turned to see Sue, who was now looking past her, trying to see what she was looking at. Emily made a motion for her to be quiet then took her to the seats at the back of the coffee shop where they could see Michael and Lauren, but Michael and Lauren couldn't see them.

"My turn to get the coffees," said Sue. She walked right past Michael, on the way there and back, not noticing him either time. She put the coffees on the table and sat. "Now, can you tell me what is going on?" she asked confused.

"Slowly look to your right, past the entrance, past the partition, and look who is there."

Sue did what she asked then quickly turned to Emily. "Michael," she whispered then looked over again. "Who's the pretty blonde?"

"Lauren!"

"Lauren?" asked Sue thinking for a moment. "His ex?"

Emily nodded her head.

"Are you positive?"

"Well, he called her Lauren."

"Are you sure?"

"Pretty sure, plus he hugged her and kissed her on the cheek. Then I heard him say that it's been a while. She talked to about him taking a trip to visit her and he said he would like that."

"A trip where?"

"I'm guessing, California."

"California! Why would he go there and leave you?"

Emily suddenly realized Sue didn't know. "A lot has happened since last time we talked."

"I thought last week was a doozy, I have a feeling this week is easily going to top that," said Sue enthusiastically, then noticed Emily's eyes watering. "Are you okay?" she asked, holding her hand.

"I'll be fine," replied Emily as she took a deep breath. She then told Sue about Brad mentioning the roses and college information in front of Michael, and how she talked to Michael the next day explaining the reason why she didn't tell him.

Sue just shook her head at Brad's antics.

"That same night Brad showed up asking about the roses and college information, I had told Michael, Ava and I were going to have a girl's night. So, now he thinks I lied to him because Brad is there talking about us going out for dinner."

"What did you do?"

"The same day we talked, I also had to explain to him about Brad showing up out of the blue, and the reason I invited him to McDonald's. It was the truth and Michael believed me."

"So, you two sorted everything out the next day, with the roses, college, dinner, and everything was fine."

"Yeah," she replied. Then she told Sue about Brad's conversation with her at McDonald's.

"That piece of...work," said Sue shaking her head disapprovingly. "Tell me you didn't buy what that snake was selling you?"

Emily was quiet.

Sue quickly noticed her silence. "What did Michael say?

"I never told him about the conversation Brad had with me," she said sheepishly.

Sue sat upright. "Why wouldn't you tell him?"

"I wanted to get those other things sorted out first. It just wasn't the right time to bring that up and I really wasn't ready to talk about it."

"Brad can tell you what he thinks, but you don't give Michael the chance to tell you what he thinks, that is so unfair," said Sue unhappy with her friend's decision. "You should have told him."

"I know that now," said Emily holding back her tears.

Sue could sense something bad happened. "Girl, what did you do?"

Emily told Sue about Michael asking how often Brad and her texted, their conversation about the content of her texts, and their intimacy.

"Why did he ask you that?

"I'm not sure," replied Emily pondering her question. "Maybe he wants to know what Brad and I do when he is not around, if we are intimate, and send intimate texts."

"There's no, maybe," said Sue bluntly.

Emily smiled at her straightforwardness. Then she told her about the conversation she had with Debbie.

"Debbie is right on the money there!" said Sue in agreement. "What did she think about Brad's words of wisdom?"

"I didn't tell her either," she said shamefully.

"You didn't tell her either! Why wouldn't you confide in her? She's your sister!"

"I was confused and tired. I wanted some time to think about it," she explained as she looked at the coffee she was drinking, rather than at Sue.

Sue noticed her friend's uneasiness. "I understand," said Sue reassuringly, "sometimes you need time to figure things out."

Emily looked up at her and told her how different and distant Michael had been acting, and how Debbie had noticed it also.

"Ava too?"

"No, Michael has been fine with her."

Sue realized it was just Emily that Michael was shunning.

She then told her how tired and irritable she was on Sunday night after work and the pursuing argument she had with Michael.

Sue sat back in her chair and put her hands on either side of her face in total disbelief. "What were you thinking?"

"I know, I know, I messed up!"

"You messed up big!" confirmed Sue. "What did you do to fix it?"

Emily told her the story about her lying in bed that night. "Then it hit me."

"What?" asked Sue leaning forward. "What hit you?"

She proceeded to tell Sue about the conversation she had with Brad yesterday afternoon.

"I'm glad you figured that all out, and told Brad, what was what!" exclaimed Sue glad to hear Brad was out of the picture for good. "What about Michael?"

"I called and texted him to meet me, but he refused, and said maybe in a few days."

"And?"

"I came up with an idea."

"What idea?" asked Sue curiously.

"Before we had our argument, he was supposed to be taking care of Ava after school today. In my second last text to him yesterday, I asked if he was still going to watch Ava."

"Let me guess, he said yes, and whenever else you need him to."

She gave Sue a puzzled look. "How did you know?"

"Really! Are you are really asking me that question?" she said, determined not to answer her.

"That's the kind of guy he is," replied Emily.

"Yes, and a hell of a lot more!" added Sue. "Now, continue with your idea."

"I thought after I came home from work today, I wouldn't let him leave till he heard me out," she explained, then looked over at Michael and Lauren laughing. "But now—"

"You see him with his ex-girlfriend and making plans to go to California," finished Sue looking over at them too.

They watched as Michael and Lauren stood up smiling. Michael helped Lauren on with her coat and held the door open as they walked outside then put his arm around her. Emily watched Michael till he walked out of view.

"They do look cozy," commented Sue turning to Emily who had tears streaming down her face. Sue moved next to her, passed her a napkin, and comforted her. "Don't you think you should talk to him, explain everything, and tell him what you saw today?"

Emily nodded no. "I want him to be happy."

"Okay," replied Sue not agreeing with her answer. "Why don't you think about it a little more?"

"I will," replied Emily.

They left the coffee shop and went to work; it was busy, so time flew. Emily worked through the dinner rush and was home by seven. As she approached the front door, she could hear Ava and Michael laughing inside, took a deep breath, and went inside.

"Mommy," shouted Ava giving her a hug.

Hi, honey," she replied hugging her back. "Hi, Michael," said Emily as cheerfully as she could.

"Hi, Emily," he replied, giving her a half smile.

"You two must have been having a good time, I could hear you laughing from the driveway."

"We were playing hide and go seek," she explained.

"Did you find any good hiding places?" asked Emily tickling her.

"I did," replied Ava laughing.

"I should get going," said Michael quietly reaching for his coat.

"You're not staying for a while with me and Mom?"

"No, I eh…"

"He has things he needs to do, Christmas things. Besides, I want some time alone with you missy," interjected Emily.

"Okay," said Ava giving Michael a big squeeze.

"Ava has a playdate after school, so I will be picking her up after I finish work tomorrow," she explained.

"That sounds like so much fun," said Michael to Ava as he put on his coat.

"There are three of us are going over there to play."

"Wow, three of you are going over there! I wouldn't like to be that mom with the four of you running around," Michael joked.

"I'm still going to your place this Friday, right?" asked Ava.

"This Friday?" asked Michael, pretending he had forgotten.

"This Friday, the twenty-third, your niece, nephews, decorating, pizza, candies, sleepover, remember?"

Michael wasn't sure what to say and quickly glanced over at Emily.

"Of course, you are," answered Emily. "Right, Michael?"

"Hmm," said Michael as he bent down looking at Ava pretending to be thinking about his answer. "I guess so."

"You know so," she replied giving him a hug before running off into the kitchen to get a drink.

"Thank you," said Michael to Emily.

"She has been looking forward to this since you told her," said Emily. "You can pick her up around three thirty."

"That's fine," he replied.

"I'll pack an overnight bag for her," she said opening the door, "and I will see you then, bye."

"Bye."

She quickly closed the door, stuck her head in the kitchen telling Ava she would be back in a minute then went into her bedroom and sat on the edge of her bed, and started to cry. Emily now wondered if Sue was right, maybe she should have talked to him, explained everything, and told him what she had witnessed at the coffee shop.

Michael walked down the driveway totally confused. Yesterday she had sent a voicemail and numerous texts asking him to meet for a talk, and there he was at her house with a prime opportunity for her to do so, and instead, she shut the door in my face.

Chapter 35

Emily was at work early; she hadn't slept well and needed to get out of the house. On the way she picked up a coffee for her and Sue and sat with her at the bar drinking them.

"How did it go last night after work?"

Emily told her.

"You stuck with your decision not to talk to him then."

"After he left, I thought maybe I should have."

"Right now, you're keeping him in the dark, and the more days that go by the further he will move away from you."

"Maybe permanently" she said miserably, "to California."

"Do you want Lauren to start getting friendly with him?" asked Sue. "I can hear it all now. Michael, I made a mistake. Can we give us a second chance? You can write in California, and we can be together," said Sue. "You know it's hip in California to be dating an out of work writer!"

"It is?" asked Emily a little unsure.

"I don't know, I just made that up, but it wouldn't surprise me if it is!" said Sue giggling before turning to Emily and becoming serious. "The question is, do you want to give Lauren that chance to reconcile?"

"Do you think he would get back together with her and move to California to be with her?

"You hurt him really good," she replied, "and someone like Lauren, comforting and consoling him, has rebound written all over it."

Emily put her head on the bar. "What have I done?"

"Can I give you a piece of advice?"

Emily moved her head sideways and looked up at her. "Sure."

"You need to stop worrying about Lauren. Start thinking about you and Michael and do something."

"Do what exactly?"

"You love him, fight for him! Tell him how you feel, tell him everything!" she said firmly. "If he loves you, he will forgive you."

"And if he doesn't?"

"Then at the very least, you know you tried."

Emily knew Sue was right.

Work was slow and the seconds ticked by like minutes; Emily couldn't wait to leave. Eventually five o'clock arrived, she got in her car, picked up Ava, and listened to her talk about her playdate. At home they made dinner, sat, and ate.

"Mom."

"Yes, Ava?"

"I miss Michael not being here," she said.

"You do. Why?"

"He makes me laugh and feel good," she replied. "He makes you laugh and feel good, too. He also makes you smile a lot."

Emily looked at her daughter.

"You look sad, Mom. Do you miss him as much as I do?"

"Very much," she replied.

"Maybe we can invite him over on Christmas Eve?" she asked.

"I'm sure his family will want him to be with them."

"Can't we ask anyway?" she said." It wouldn't hurt to ask him. Ms. Smith told us in class today, that if you don't ask, you will never find out the answer."

"We'll see, maybe," replied Emily and thought about what Ava's teacher had said.

After they finished dinner, they watched a movie, and Emily let Ava stay up a little later than usual to keep her company then put her to bed. She looked at the phone, I should call him and ask him to meet me tomorrow, she thought. She picked it up, put it down, and then picked it up again. "No!" she said out loud, putting the phone down. "Change of plan! Tomorrow morning I'm going over to see him."

Michael moped around the house most of the day. He knew what Emily had said was cruel and hurtful, but she didn't seem to be herself; something had been bothering her. After dinner, he thought about sending her a text to meet tomorrow to talk about it, the only thing stopping him was the uncertainty that she may have actually meant what she had said. Maybe Brad was the person she needed to be with, not him, so he decided against it. Michael noticed the folder on his dresser and decided to continue reading Emily's short stories. By midnight, he finished the last one then went to bed.

Chapter 36

At nine o'clock Michael's phone rang. "Hello."

"Are you doing anything today?" asked the voice on the other end.

"No, no plans."

"I need to do some last-minute Christmas shopping. Do you want to come with me?"

"I would like that."

"I'll pick you up in an hour."

"See you in an hour," he reconfirmed.

Emily walked out the door a few minutes before ten, she was determined that he was going to listen to what she had to say, whether he wanted to hear it or not. She walked down her street and turned onto his. In the distance she watched a car pull over, Lauren get out, and walk around the back of the car onto the sidewalk. As soon as she did, Michael appeared, gave her a hug, and they jumped into the car. Emily watched them drive away, then turned around, and slowly walked home with tears running down her face. Once inside, she went upstairs to bed, and didn't come down again till it was time to pick up Ava.

Chapter 37

Michael knocked on Emily's door at three thirty.

She opened it. "Ava will be out in a minute," she said closing the door on him.

Michael was taken back by what she did and waited.

The door opened and Ava came out "Michael!" she screamed. "I can't wait! This is going to be so much fun!"

Emily came out, kissed Ava goodbye, then handed Michael her overnight bag. "Tomorrow, drop her off at work at five," she said coldly before closing the door.

They walked to Michael's house, dropped off Ava's bag, and then drove to his parents' house. Inside Ava met Michael's parents, Jenny, her brothers, Aaron, and Nick, and then took off to play with them. Michael was talking with his parents, when his cell suddenly beeped, it was a Gmail. As he read it his face lit up.

"Everything okay?" asked his mother.

"Yes," he replied cheerfully, "I will be back in an hour." He started for home, halfway there he realized he could have driven and decided to continue on foot. Inside his apartment he turned on his laptop, opened up his Gmail, and printed it off the message along with the attached file. He put the documents into a big envelope and walked out the door.

After Emily closed the door on Michael, she felt awful about what she had just done, and was about to go upstairs when her phone beeped. It was a text from Brad asking if he could pick her up in fifteen for a quick coffee. She wasn't in the mood, but remembered she was the one that had mentioned it to Brad about seeing him before he left today, so she agreed to go. She quickly got ready then waited for him in front of her house.

Inside the coffee shop, Brad told her he had bought the condo and that he was moving in the first week of January. Emily congratulated him.

"I thought about what you said to me the other day, about me meeting someone that is more into my lifestyle, I think you're right. I enjoy what I do, I like travelling, I love working in the city, and soon I'll to be living there," he said with a grin. "I do need to meet someone who also wants that, so I was thinking in January, I would ask Chloe out. You remember her, you met her at the party."

"I do, she was very beautiful and sociable, and she really likes you," replied Emily. "I'm sure she would love to do all those things with you."

Brad noticed she hadn't mentioned anything about Michael and decided not to ask. "Ava must be excited about Christmas?"

"She is ecstatic," replied Emily. "Tonight, she is staying at Michael's for a sleepover. His niece and two nephews are going to be there also. From what Michael told me; they are going to have a blast."

After hearing her mention Michael, Brad assumed she had spoken with him, and they had worked everything out. He was happy for both of them. "I'm sure they'll have a great time," he said looking at her, "he's a wonderful guy."

"He is," she replied nervously. "Ava thinks he's the best."

Emily listened as Brad talked about staying with his parents, moving to his new place, and admitting he would miss the town but was looking forward to city life. After they finished their coffees, Brad pulled up in front of Emily's house and walked with her to the front door.

"I'm happy for you and Ava," he said sincerely. "Michael is a special guy and he's very fortunate to have you two in his life."

"Thank you," she said stopping close to it.

"Have a great Christmas, and make sure you tell Ava and Michael, that also."

"I will," she replied, "and you have a lovely Christmas with your family."

"Thank you," replied Brad. "If there is anything you three need, I'm only a phone call away," he offered genuinely.

"Thank you, I appreciate that."

They hugged, Brad kissed her on the cheek, and then they each turned around and went their separate ways.

Michael walked onto his street then turned onto Emily's. He was too busy thinking about the contents of the envelope to spot the car pulling up in front of Emily's house, and the people getting out. When he arrived at her driveway, he turned to go up it, and suddenly stopped. Emily was walking up the side of the house with Brad. He watched them stop, Brad say something, them hug, and then Brad kissing her on the cheek. Michael turned around and quickly left. He arrived at his house, thought about just dropping the envelope off and going to his parents. Instead, he decided to walk to Emily's work and wait for her there. Ten minutes later Emily pulled up, got out of her car, and strolled to the front of the bar.

"Emily," he called out.

"Michael!" she replied surprised. "Is everything okay? Is Ava okay?"

"Yes, she is fine, she's at my parents playing with my niece and nephews."

From inside the bar Sue noticed them. "This should be interesting," she said to herself.

"What are you doing here?"

"I wanted to show you this," he said handing her the envelope.

"What is it?" she asked taking it from him. "What's inside?"

"Take a look," he replied.

She took out the documents, read the Gmail and screamed. "They are going to publish your story!" She was so excited for him. She grabbed him, held him close, and whispered, "I'm so happy for you. This is amazing. What a perfect Christmas present!"

"This looks promising," said Sue not realizing she was moving closer to the window.

"I received the Gmail an hour ago I wanted you to be the first to know."

"No one else knows?" she asked surprised.

"Nope, you're the first."

"Thanks," she said, flattered. "What's this other document?"

"My contract," he said, "look at this here."

"They are paying you an advance?"

"Yep," he smiled. "It's not much but enough for a trip." He didn't mean to say that.

Emily handed back the envelope and the documents. "A trip...Oh, let's see, somewhere like…California?" she asked, terribly upset.

"This doesn't look good," admitted Sue.

"California?" asked Michael startled.

"Don't look so surprised Michael, I saw you this morning with Lauren, and on Tuesday."

"What are you talking about?"

"Keep on denying it," she said. "What, you didn't think you wouldn't get caught sneaking around with her! I was with Sue, and she saw you two together also."

"I…" He realized arguing with her was pointless. "Why do you care?"

His question caught her off guard and she tried to think of a quick response.

"This coming from the person who was hugging and making out with Brad by her front door."

"What? When?" she asked. "You don't know what you are talking about!"

"Before I came here, I went to your place first and as I turn onto your driveway, there you two are," he explained.

"No, no, no! Hold on, that's not what happened."

"It doesn't matter anyway, does it?" he said as he turned to walk away. "You made your decision!"

"You did too! Enjoy California!" she yelled at him. Emily was too upset to go inside; instead, she went to the side of the building leaned against the wall and put her hands on her head then bent forward.

"Are you okay?" asked Sue zipping up her coat.

She was going to say she was fine but told her the truth. "No, not really."

"What was all that about?" she asked curiously.

Emily told her.

"He came all the way here to tell you his book was published and told you before anyone else. You don't think that's odd?"

"Odd, in what way?"

"Why would he do that?" queried Sue. "Why would he track you down, let you be the first to hear his good news, and want to celebrate it with you? Why didn't he tell Lauren first?" asked Sue shaking her head at her friend's blindness. "That man is head over heels for you, girl."

"I thought the same thing, too," she said removing her hands and looking up at sky. "Until he mentioned the trip, then I lost it."

"Maybe he meant a trip for you, him, and Ava. Did you ever think about that?"

"I don't believe he meant us," she whispered.

"Now you can read his mind?"

"What's that supposed to mean" she asked defensively.

"You're talking about what you think you know and believing it to be the truth. If you would have talked to him the other day and today, you would know truth, instead of fabricating what you think to be true."

Emily went quiet.

Sue put her arm around her.

"He was so excited about his book being published," said Emily sadly, "and I ruined one of the happiest days of his life. I feel so awful."

"Yes, you did," agreed Sue, "and you should feel awful."

"Sue! You are supposed to be on my side."

"Emily, I'm your friend and I'll always have your back, but I will never lie to you."

Emily smiled. "I know that's what I love about you!"

"So, are you going to fix this?"

"Yes, I am."

"When?"

"When he drops Ava off tomorrow, I will ask if he wants to come over later to talk."

"You're doing the right thing," said Sue assuredly.

"Thanks for being there for me," said Emily as they started walking to the entrance of the bar.

"I will always be here for you," verified Sue.

I hope he agrees to come over tomorrow night, thought Emily as they walked inside, she didn't know what else she to do if he said no.

Michael gloomily walked away from the bar wondering what had happened. He arrived home, put the envelope in his bedroom, and then left for his parents. Before going inside, he put what had happened out of his mind; tonight, was for the kids.

Chapter 38

Michael stayed for thirty minutes before rounding up the children and putting them in his car. After they pulled up to the local Christmas tree lot, he turned to the children, saying, "what we need to do, is find a tree that no one will ever pick or want, and give it a home for Christmas."

They jumped out of the car and walked around the lot till they found the tree they were looking for. It was missing branches, had bare spots, and was slightly lopsided.

"Are you sure you want this one?" asked the attendant looking at Michael.

Michael looked at the children. "What is I kids? It's…"

"Perfect!" they shouted.

"We're going to give it a good home for Christmas," said Jenny. "Right Ava?"

"Yes, we are!" Ava confirmed. "We are going to decorate it from top to bottom, and it's going to look beautiful."

"That's nice of your kids to take a tree like this and give it a home for Christmas," said the attendant cheerfully. "Let me do my part to help you out, and give it to you, no charge."

"Yeah!" shouted the children.

"What's your name?" asked Aaron to the attendant.

"It's Jack Bear, but because of my last name and this long beard, my friends call me Grizzly."

Aaron gathered the other children in a huddle, they whispered back and forth, Michael looked over at Grizzly and shrugged his shoulders as if to say, "I have no idea what they are up to." The children eventually broke out of their huddle.

"In honor of you, we are going to name our tree," said Aaron, then turned to the others and counted down, "three, two, one."

"Grizzly!" the children screamed.

Grizzly laughed. "Well, that is awfully kind of you kids to do that for me, thank you, and Merry Christmas!"

"Merry Christmas!" yelled the children. They picked up the tree and walked to the car chanting, "Grizzly! Grizzly! Grizzly!"

"Those are fine children you have there," said Grizzly, "Merry Christmas."

"Thank you," replied Michael shaking his hand, "Merry Christmas."

They tied the tree to the top of the car, drove to Michael's house, then carried it inside and placed it in the stand in the far corner of the living room. On the dining room table were all the items the children needed to make decoration for the tree and the living room. The children sat around the table and began while Michael ordered pizzas. When the pizzas came, they took a break, and then returned to the table to finish their individual decorations. Once they had, they all worked together to make the star for the top of the tree. After they finished, they decorated the tree with their ornaments, put the lights around it, and Michael lifted Ava up to put the star on top. Then they counted down from ten; when they hit zero, Michael plugged in the lights, and they all cheered as the tree lit up. Now it was time to decorate the room, when they were done, they all stood around and admired their work.

"Okay, guys, pajama-time," said Michael.

The boys got changed in the spare room, while the girls changed in Michael's. When they came out, Michael had placed several blankets and pillows in front of the television and on the two couches. The two girls took the floor while the boys took a couch each. Michael then made them hot chocolates with marshmallows, as well as buttered popcorn, and put the candies in a big bowl and gave it to them, before finding a place on the floor next to the girls. They all got comfortable, watched Christmas movies, and one by one the children fell asleep. Michael covered them with blankets, went to his room, got under the sheets, and fell asleep.

Emily had an extremely busy night at work and didn't get home till two; she was exhausted. She went upstairs, got ready for bed, and was asleep by the time her head hit the pillow.

Chapter 39

Emily woke up at nine, got ready for work, then made a coffee and a toasted bagel. She had a good night's sleep and was in a pleasant mood. She contemplated why and realized it was because she was going to ask Michael to talk tonight and hopefully straighten everything out. The only issue, and it was a big one, was that it was Christmas Eve. At ten, she grabbed her coat and car keys, suddenly her phone beeped, it was a text from Michael, and she excitedly read it: "Good morning, Mommy, having a lot of fun, love Ava." She smiled at her message as she left her house and strolled to her car.

"Are you still going to ask him tonight to talk?" asked Sue as Emily walked into the bar.

"Definitely," she replied with an air of confidence. "I was thinking about what you said yesterday and you're right. I don't know what's going on and I need answers."

"That's more like it," said Sue encouragingly, "and it is Christmas Eve, the magical night when wishes come true, so anything can happen."

Emily thought about that, Christmas Eve wishes, and decided to make one. "I wish to see Michael later on tonight, that we talk, resolve everything, and are together forever," she said quietly to herself.

The day was steady, and it would have gone by a lot quicker if she hadn't kept on checking the time. Finally, it was ten minutes to five. She did her cash out, finished her cleaning, and did one final walk behind the bar and around the dining area before grabbing her handbag and heading to the bathroom to freshen up. She fixed her hair, put on lipstick, and looked at herself in the mirror. "You can do this," she said with as much confidence as she could muster.

Michael had been listening to the children giggling in the living room for a while when all of a sudden it went quiet. The bedroom door suddenly swung open, and the four children screamed as they jumped on the bed, each trying to get close to him. Nick started shouting, "Wake up! Wake up!" and the others joined in. When they stopped, Aaron started shouting, "Hungry! Hungry!" and the others joined in again. They pulled Michael out of bed, into the kitchen, where he prepared four bowls of cereal and placed them on the floor in front of the television. As they ate, he cleaned off the clippings from the dining room table then picked up the empty cups and bowls from last night and soaked them in the sink. Once the children had finished, he added their cereal bowls, and did the dishes and looked on as the children watched cartoons. At ten, he gave Ava his phone and helped her text her mom and did the same with Jenny. Then Michael and the children watched a Christmas movie after which they played games for a while. Around lunchtime they helped Michael make pancake batter then cheered as they watched him flip the pancakes from the frying pan. As they ate, Michael listened to them excitedly talk about Santa coming tonight. When they'd finished, they all looked outside at the fresh fallen snow.

"Do you guys want to go outside and play?"

"Yes," they screamed.

"Okay, keep your pajamas on, and put your snow pants jackets over them," he explained and helped them get ready. Pulling the curtain and patio door aside, one by one the children walked outside and into the backyard. He left the door slightly open so he could hear them play while he prepared the buffet dinner for his family. After a couple of hours, Michael called them in, and helped them remove their outdoor clothes then hung them up to dry. As they drank hot chocolate, the children talked about the snow forts, and snowmen they had built.

"Girls grab your bags and go into my room, boys grab yours and go into the spare room, it's time to change out of your pajamas and into your Christmas Eve clothes." The girls excitedly ran into the room to put on their dresses, the boys somewhat less enthusiastic, sauntered into theirs. Once dressed, Michael took pictures of them by 'Grizzly the Christmas Tree.'

Suddenly, there was a knock at the door, and Michael answered it. A courier handed him an envelope, which he signed for, then said Merry Christmas and left. He opened the envelope, read the letter, and let out a jubilant yell. The children excited by his scream, came over and watched him as he took a black marker and wrote a note on the outside of the envelope, and then helped him wrap it. He placed it on the dining room table next to a card.

A short time later his parents, sister, and her husband arrived. They listened as the children talked about their night and day. At four forty-five, Michael picked up the card, the wrapped envelope, and looked on as Ava said goodbye.

Chapter 40

Michael drove Ava to her mom's work, parked the car, and walked with her towards the entrance.

"I was having so much fun," said Ava. "Do you think me, and Mom can go back to your place?"

Michael wasn't sure what to say. "Your mom may have other plans," he suggested. "It's Christmas Eve."

"But if she doesn't?" she asked hopefully.

"We'll see," he replied as they walked to the front door. Michael noticed Emily walking around the dining room, grabbing her bag and heading in the direction of the bathroom. Michael opened the door and sat Ava on the stool. "You tell your mom to open these straight away, the little one first, then the big one next," he instructed her as he placed them on the bar, "and tell her they're early Christmas presents."

"I will," said Ava. "Can you send me the pictures from last night and today so I can show my mom?"

"I'll send them to your mom's phone as soon as I get home," he promised as he hugged her. "Merry Christmas, Ava."

"Merry Christmas, Michael," she replied watching him leave.

A minute later Emily walked out of the bathroom surprised to see Ava sitting alone.

"Hi, Mom," she said merrily.

"Hi, honey. Where's Michael?" she asked in a panic.

"He just left," she answered.

"Left! Oh no!" she said running outside. In the distance she watched his car drive away. So much for Christmas Eve wishes, she thought, as she sadly went inside. "Did you have a good time?" she asked walking behind the bar.

"I had so much fun!"

Sue, who had been hiding in the back office, came out to the front, and stood next to Emily. "What did he say?" she asked anxiously.

"I didn't get the chance to talk to him I was in the bathroom. He came in, dropped Ava off, and left."

"He left!" cried Sue.

"What am I going to do now?" asked Emily putting her head on the bar and noticing the envelopes. "Did you get presents Ava?" she asked raising her head.

"No, these are for you. Michael said to open the little one first, then the big one. He said they're early Christmas presents."

Emily looked at Sue.

"Don't look at me, open them!" she said excitedly.

Emily picked up the small envelope, opened it, and removed a sheet of paper. It was folded in half and there was a note that she read to herself: 'Everyone will know.' After she unfolded it, on top was another note: 'I added this when I sent in my manuscript, it will be within the first few pages of my book.' Her eyes moved down to the typed words in the middle of the paper, and she happily smiled.

"What is it Mom?"

"Yeah, what is it?" asked Sue.

She read the two notes aloud.

"And?" asked Sue.

She read the typed words: "'Acknowledgments,' and underneath, 'My Editor, Emily Anderson.'" She looked over at Sue. "The night I had words with him I told him if his book gets published, no one would ever know it was me that had edited it. When he sent his manuscript in two weeks ago, he must have added this to it. He didn't tell me, even when I said no one would ever know it was me, he still didn't let on. When his book is published this is going to be within the first few pages of his novel. Do you believe it?"

"I do, you deserve it," said Sue "Congratulations!"

"Thank you," said Emily as she picked up the big envelope. "Did Michael wrap this?"

"We all did," clarified Ava, "Michael, me, Jenny, Aaron, Nick."

Emily took the wrapping off. "A Federal Express envelope," she said a little surprised. She read the note on the outside written in black marker out loud: "It was addressed to me, but it is meant for you, Michael." She looked over at Ava. "Did this get delivered today?"

"This afternoon, when Michael opened it, he made this happy yell," she said copying him. "Then he wrote the note and asked us to help him wrap it."

Emily took the two documents and began to read the first: "To Emily Anderson, a few weeks ago we received a manuscript sent via Gmail from Michael. A few days later I received, by courier, a copy of the printed manuscript that you had edited. After my editors read Michael's manuscript, we agreed this was the one we are going to go with. My senior editor declared the manuscript was flawless and questioned me whether or not Michael had edited it himself or had used someone else. I recalled Michael having sent me your edited copy and retrieved it. Michael had put a note with that same document explaining who you were and your background. I passed the note, plus the edited manuscript, onto my senior editor. He reviewed your work and was so impressed with what he saw that he suggested I hire you. Which brings me to the reason for this letter. Attached you will find an offer for a letter of employment, please read through it carefully. With this position, you will be able to work from home, but you will be expected to videoconference into our monthly meetings, and fly to New York several times throughout the year, all expenses paid, of course. Our office is closed over the holidays and is reopening January 3, please take your time to review our offer, and we look forward to hearing your response in early January. My deepest apologies for not sending this information directly to you, regards Peter Paterson." She looked up at Sue. "I can't believe it! I can't believe it!" she shouted, jumping up and down. Sue joined in, and Ava climbed off her stool, ran around the bar, and jumped up and down with them.

"Read the other," said Sue ecstatically, "read the other one."

Emily read the offer to herself then paraphrased it. "Basically, it says they want me start full time at the end of January, it lists my responsibilities, such as editing, proofreading, etc." She gave them an astonished look. "I don't believe it, if I sign it, they will give me full credit for editing Michael's book and pay me for editing it. They will give me this amount once I sign," she said showing Sue.

"Wow!" exclaimed Sue.

Emily continued. "It says I have till January 6 to accept." Emily read the rest to herself, then looked up; she was speechless as she pointed out her salary to Sue.

Sue was flabbergasted.

Emily screamed, Sue screamed, Ava screamed, and once again they all cheerfully jumped up and down. When they stopped Emily put the documents back in the envelope with a sad look.

"What's wrong?" asked Sue.

"I want to run over and celebrate with Michael, but I can't," she said holding back her tears.

"Don't you think maybe you should?" advised Sue. "He at least deserves a thank you."

"He has Lauren, his trip, and his life," she said as her phone started beeping crazily. "What the…?" she asked reaching for her phone. "It's multiple texts from Michael and they're all pictures."

"I asked him to send me pictures from last night and today," explained Ava impatiently, "let me see them."

Emily lifted Ava onto the bar. As Emily showed them, Ava explained them, as Sue looked on. There were several pictures of Ava with Jenny, then the four of them making decorations, and eating pizza.

"Oh that's, 'Grizzly the Christmas Tree,' said Ava.

"Grizzly the Christmas Tree?" asked Emily.

Ava told them the story which made Emily and Sue laugh, then continued to describe the pictures. "Here is one of Grizzly decorated…this is Michael's house decorated…the snowmen we made in his backyard…and the fort we built…me, Jenny, Aaron, Nick, all dressed up in front of Grizzly…a picture of Michael and Laur—"

"I don't believe it!" said Emily cutting Ava off and frowning. "She was there?" asked Emily pointing to Lauren.

"Yes."

"Friday and Saturday?" asked Emily.

"No, just Saturday," replied Ava "She's really nice."

Emily was hurt by Ava's comment. "You like Lauren."

"Who is Lauren?" asked Ava confused.

"This girl in the picture," said Emily pointing, "Michael's girlfriend, her name is Lauren."

"That's not his girlfriend" replied Ava, "and her name is Laura."

"Trust me it will be soon," she implied, "and you must have heard it wrong honey, it's Lauren."

The next picture was Michael, Lauren, and another man.

"Who is this man?" Emily asked.

"That's David."

"David?" asked Emily. "Who is David?"

"David is Laura's husband," she revealed.

Emily had this awful feeling come over her. "Laura is?"

"Laura is Michael's sister," she said cheerfully. "Actually, her name is Laura-Anne, but everyone calls her Laura, except for Michael when he's out in public with her. He calls her Laura-Anne to embarrass her. Oh, and guess what?"

Emily was afraid to ask. "What?"

"Laura and David had a Jell-O wedding cake!" she said laughing hysterically.

Emily looked at Sue. "Her name is Laura-Anne, it's his sister." At first, she had this horrified look on her face for mistaking Laura-Anne for Lauren, but after she thought for a moment, a radiant smile came on her face as it sunk in. "There is no Lauren, no trip to California, and no one else," she said out loud.

"I told you, you should have talked to him," said Sue shaking her head and grinning at her friend. "What you going to do now?"

"Ava, where is Michael?"

"At his house."

"Do you want to go see him?"

"Yes!" she shrieked putting her arms out to be lifted down then running for the door.

Emily picked up her envelopes, put her arms around Sue, and said, "Merry Christmas,"

"Merry Christmas," replied Sue. "Go get him, girl."

"Merry Christmas Sue," said Ava.

"Merry Christmas, Ava," replied Sue.

Emily drove to her house and quickly changed. She picked up her envelope from underneath the tree, put it with the other two, and then they walked to Michael's house. Outside, Emily asked Ava to wait a minute while she composed herself, then told her to knock on the door.

Chapter 41

David opened the door.

"Hi, I'm Emily, is Michael here?" she asked nervously.

"Come in, and let me take your coats," said David. "Hi, Ava, nice to see you again,"

"You too," she replied.

"Ava!" shouted Jenny excitedly running to her, grabbing her hand, and taking off.

"Michael hasn't come back yet from dropping Ava off," said David somewhat confused and wondering where he was.

"His car was in the driveway," Emily explained, "I thought he might be here." She hadn't anticipated his family being there.

"That's odd," said Laura walking up to Emily with the feeling they had met before. "I'm sure he will be here soon, please come in, and meet everyone. I'm Laura, Michael's sister, this is David my husband," she said pleasantly and leading her into the living room. "I'm finally glad to put a face to the name. Michael never stops talking about you."

"All good I hope," she said timidly.

"Of course," replied Laura. "This is my mom Beth, my father Richard, and this pretty little girl here is Jenny, and those two over there are Aaron and Nick."

"Hello," said Emily.

"We've heard so much about you," said Beth. "I'm so glad we finally get to meet you."

"Michael said you were beautiful," added Richard, "but looking at you now, I realize he was being modest."

"Thank you," replied Emily shyly, "that's very sweet of you."

"Would you like a drink?" asked David.

"A beer, please," she replied as she watched him leave to grab one, and a couple of shots, she thought.

"I'm sorry," said David apologetically. "Do you want a glass?"

"This is fine, thank you," she replied taking a sip from the bottle.

"I'm sure he will be here shortly," assured Richard, "please, have a seat."

She was about to, when the door opened, it was Michael.

"Sorry everyone, I had to run a quick errand," he said closing the door behind him and taking off his coat before noticing her. "Emily!" he said surprised to see her.

"Hi, Michael, I hope you don't mind?" she asked feeling embarrassed for showing up uninvited.

Michael could see she felt awkward and immediately put her mind at ease. "I'm glad you made it," he said walking over to her. "Did you meet everyone?"

"I did," she said, smiling as she looked around at them, then back at Michael. She had to tell him now. "I need to talk to you," she whispered. Everyone, except the children who were playing in the corner, was looking at them.

"Okay," said Michael. "We can go into my room?"

In most circumstances, she thought that would have been the best thing to do, but with him telling his family so much about her, she felt that they needed to hear what she had to say too. "I think what I have to say, I need to say in front of your family. I owe one of them an apology, actually two of them," she said correcting herself. "Unless you don't want to hear a story about Michael and me?" she asked reservedly looking at them.

"Are you kidding? A story about my brother and a beautiful girl I'm all ears," said Laura sitting up on the couch.

"We love good stories, look at who we have in our family," said Beth looking over at Michael the storyteller, "Although I must admit, the only problem with his stories are they are always fictional, never about him, so please, tell us."

Emily looked over at Michael. "Are you okay with this?"

"I am," he said encouraging her, "don't worry, I'll help you out if you get stuck."

She was glad to hear that.

Before she started, Michael took the kids into his bedroom, put on a movie, and gave them candy, While David filled up everyone's drink then sat down next to Laura.

"That will keep them busy," said Michael standing with Emily in front of his family.

Emily moved over close to him and began. She told them about the first time they met at the bar. How he walked her home, talked about his book, and how she agreed to read and edit it. How the following day, when he came into her work to drop off the manuscript, he offered to sit with Ava, and how sweet and charming he was. And him coming over to babysit Ava, while she went to a Christmas party with Brad, and what Brad had said in the car about penniless writers. About the lame party, then coming home, eating cold pizza, drinking beer, and laughing with Michael. "He told me this amazing story about this wedding he went to," she said quickly describing it. "At first, I didn't know whether to believe him or not, he said he had pictures, so I did." She looked over at Laura and David. "He didn't tell me whose wedding it was. This evening, after he dropped Ava off, she told me it was you wedding and that you were the couple that had the Jell-O wedding cake."

"Why didn't you tell her it was our wedding?" questioned Laura mischievously looking at Michael.

"She'd only just met me, I didn't want to scare her away by saying it was my sister's wedding, and thinking my family was crazy," he replied then looked at Emily. "Which they are by the way!"

"Emily, that's not true," said Laura, "we're only a little crazy," making them all laugh.

"I wish I would have been there," confessed Emily, "it sounded amazing."

"Thank you, it was," replied Laura, who looked at David, and kissed him.

Emily told them about cutting down the Christmas tree, making breakfast, the Santa Claus Parade, and decorating the tree. She explained how she didn't like her job, her financial situation, and how Michael was helping her out by taking care of Ava. And all the wonderful things he had done with Ava. She then told them about them going for a walk in the Aurora Trails, about Michael telling the story of Beatrice and Robert Johnson. How Michael had told said to Robert that he had her as his editor. She intentionally left out the story about his great-aunt Carol; instead, she explained how Michael had spoken to her about Lauren and why he had moved into this place. How they took Ava to the mall to see Santa, meeting her parents, and playing pool and dancing. She told them about Brad, the roses, the college information, and the talk she had with Michael the following day. "I know Michael knows all of this, but because you all mentioned he has spoken of me to you, I wasn't sure how much he had told you. So, if none of this, I am so embarrassed, if only some of it, well now you have the complete picture."

"We've heard bits and pieces," confirmed Beth.

"I've heard most of it," said Laura trying to make her feel at ease.

She smiled at their honesty and thoughtfulness. "This next piece I am going to tell you, I know none of you know, not even Michael." Emily told them the conversation Brad had had with her in McDonald's. She faltered a couple of times but got through to the end. When she finished, she looked at Michael. "I'm so sorry I should have told you," she said with an incredibly sad look on her face, she didn't want to cry in front of them, and desperately fought back her tears.

"Why didn't you say something?" he asked compassionately.

"I don't know, Brad has that way of putting ideas and thoughts in your head, and making you believe they are true. I guess I was unsure and confused and needed time to think about it."

"I understand," said Michael, "but we could have talked it through together. I would have helped you out in January, February…all year."

"I know that now, but at the time I didn't want you to have to put your life on hold for me. I thought that would be selfish and unfair of me to do that to you," she said reaching and squeezing his hand. "I'm so sorry."

"I know," said Michael giving her a smile and not letting go of her hand.

"Brad sounds like a jerk," said Beth matter-of-fact.

"I could use more descriptive words than that mom, but we can stick with jerk for now," suggested Laura.

"You two may not want to pass judgment on him too quickly, until you hear what I said to Michael, the other day." She described in detail the argument between Michael and her. They were silent. She looked at the ground unsure what to do next.

Michael squeezed her hand gently. She looked up at him, he smiled, and whispered, "go on Emily."

With his encouragement she continued. "I know you must think I'm awful for what I said to him, and to this day, I'm so embarrassed and upset by what I said. I know I hurt him deeply, and for that I will never forgive myself." She knew that was the most difficult thing she had to tell him and them. Feeling a little more confident now, she told them about the night she was lying in bed and thinking about what she had just done to Michael, and how she came to figure out what the problem was. "This is also something that Michael doesn't know or any of you," she said and told them about her meeting with Brad, and their conversation, almost word for word.

"Why didn't you tell me this?" Michael asked.

"You don't remember?"

"No."

"I left you a voicemail and I texted you several times. You told me you wanted to wait a few days."

Michael realized he did say that. "I did. I'm sorry Emily. I wish I wouldn't have."

"It's okay, you had every right to be angry with me," she replied in his defense. "I thought the following day, when you showed up to watch Ava, I would talk to you after I got home from work. But—"

"You practically pushed me out the door."

She smiled at him. "There is a reason why," she said turning to Laura. "Do you recognize me?"

"When I saw you walking in here tonight, I knew I had met you somewhere before, but I couldn't put my finger on where. We have met, right?"

Emily nodded her head. "Wednesday morning."

Laura thought back. "At the coffee shop, you bumped into me!"

"I did," Emily confirmed.

"Wait, you were there?" asked Michael.

"I was looking for my friend Sue when I accidentally bumped into Laura. I watched her go to you and you standing up and saying Lauren."

"Lauren!" said Michael and Laura in unison.

"You thought my sister was Lauren?" he asked.

"I did, I thought you called her Lauren," said Emily, "and she is blonde and very attractive."

"Well, thank you," said Laura appreciating the compliment.

"You're welcome," replied Emily with a grin. "I'm sorry I thought you were Lauren."

"It's not all your fault, it's mostly this idiot's fault," replied Laura looking at Michael. "Remember, you called me Laura-Anne…Lauren…Laura-Anne…they sound very similar."

"I did," recalled Michael now understanding why Emily thought he was with Lauren. "So, you thought I was back with Lauren."

"I overheard you saying you hadn't seen each other for a while, something about meeting her, and going on a trip."

"That's true, Laura and I hadn't seen each other in a while," confessed Michael, "and Laura, David, and their kids are going to Florida for spring break. They said I should come down and meet them."

Emily's face went red. "I didn't realize that then, but I do now, don't I feel foolish," she said with a hopeless look.

Michael laughed and she did too.

"Oh, it gets better," she said looking around at his family and continuing. "On Friday morning, I decided I was going to come here, and that Michael was going to listen to me, no matter what, and I was determined I wasn't going to take no for an answer. So, I started to walk over to his place around ten in the morning, and as I turned the corner onto his street, I saw Lauren jump out of her car and greet Michael in front of his house. At that point, I just assumed Michael and Lauren were back together."

"As you know now, that was me?" said Laura.

"I do," replied Emily.

"Michael and I went to do some last-minute Christmas shopping at the mall," explained Laura.

"Again, I apologize for thinking you were Lauren."

"Like I said, it's not all your fault," she said looking at Michael. "It's just as much, funny man's fault her, for calling me Laura-Anne in the first place."

"I can't argue with you there, sis," agreed Michael.

Emily continued. "Michael came to my work to tell me some fantastic news." She looked over at him. "Did you tell them yet?"

"No, not yet."

She motioned with her head as if to say, "go on, tell them."

"To be quite honest with you, I was planning on telling you this tonight, and I wasn't quite sure how I was going to. But with this story unfolding here now, I think this would be the perfect opportunity to do so." He took a deep breath. "Peter Paterson is going to publish my book."

His family cheered, stood up, and congratulated him. Emily let go of his hand and took a few steps back to give them some room.

As they sat, Michael grabbed Emily's hand again, and he continued their story. "I received a Gmail yesterday, informing me, that they were going to publish my story. No offence to you guys, but the first person I wanted to tell, that I needed to tell, was Emily. So, I went to her work and told her," he said looking over at her, "and I wouldn't have done it any differently."

Emily fought back her tears.

"I also told her, that they were giving me an advance, and blurted out how it was enough for a trip. But when I say trip, Emily thinks…" he said looking over at her to answer.

"I think he means he's going on a trip to California to visit Lauren because I'm under the impression they're back together. So, I lose it. I confront him about Lauren and taking a trip to California. Which he is totally confused about," she said blushing. "Then he tells me…"

"Now I'm upset. Before I went to Emily's work, I went by her place to tell her about me being published. As I'm walking up the driveway, I see her and Brad holding each other, and making out. So, I tell her what I witnessed."

"Brad had come by to say goodbye, and he gave me a hug and a peck on the cheek. I think Michael exaggerated his point when he said we were making out to make me feel bad."

"Okay, okay, you're right," he replied, "it is true I did embellish the story for my benefit."

"We definitely have some communication issues," said Emily making them all laugh.

When the laughter died down Michael turned to Emily. "When I said trip to you at your work, I was referring to me, you and Ava going to meet Laura, David and their kids in Florida."

"Really," she said happily and put her hands over her face. The tears started to fall as Michael pulled her close to him.

"Are you okay?" he whispered.

"I'm okay," she quietly replied back.

He waited till Emily composed herself. With his arm around her, they faced his family, and Michael finished off their story. "Today, a package came, and I opened it up. I soon realized it wasn't for me but for Emily. I gave it to Ava to give to her mom," he said stopping, "Emily, you tell them."

"I received an offer for an editing position with Peter Paterson Publishers of New York, the same publishers as Michael."

Michael's family cheered again, stood up, and congratulated her. Michael removed his arm, giving her, her moment.

"I know I have been taking up so much of your time on this special night," said Emily, "and I apologize for—"

"Are you kidding me? This has been the best Christmas Eve's we have ever had!" said David honestly, and out of the blue, making them all laugh.

"A hundred times better than Michael's fictional Christmas tales," added Laura, "which put us to sleep."

"Thank you, David, Laura," replied Michael taking their teasing well.

Richard noticed Emily had something else to say. "Go ahead, dear."

"When I showed up tonight, I wasn't expecting you all to be here, but now I am glad that you are." She looked over at Michael's parents. "Beth, Richard, you have a wonderful, kind, caring, and loving son. You should be very proud of him."

"Thank you, we are," they both replied.

She turned to Michael. "I wish I could take back those awful words I said to you, but I can't. And I wish I would have spoken to you about things straight away, but I didn't. I want you to know, I will never speak poorly of you ever again or keep anything from you." She reached over and grabbed the card that she had taken from under her Christmas tree. "I wrote this card on December twentieth, before you found out about your book, and me being offered the editing position. It's my Christmas wish. Ava wrote the date on it, and to Santa, but it's actually for you."

Michael opened the card, and he laughed when he saw the cover. It was a colorful picture of Minnie Mouse kissing Mickey while she is holding a mistletoe over their heads, and Mickey is blushing. He turned around and showed it to his family. He then opened it and read the caption to everyone: "I'm the Minnie to your Mickey, Merry Christmas." He looked over at Emily. "I love this card, it's perfect."

"I thought so, too," she said. "Please, read out loud what I wrote inside."

"You told me the backbone to any couple is the unconditional love and support they give to one another, in good times, and more importantly, in bad times. I want you to know you will always have my unconditional love and support, and that you are my soulmate. My Christmas wish is that you feel the same way about me also, Love Emily." Michael stared at her deeply in thought.

She nervously looked at him, waiting for him to say or do something.

"Can you give me one second?" he asked. "I want to get the children."

Emily stood there silently on her own as his family quietly looked on. She was confused and wondered if he was bringing the children out because he didn't want to talk about this anymore or maybe because she had hurt him so badly, he didn't feel the same way as she did. Emily's thoughts were broken by his voice.

"Okay, guys," he said, "sit here on the floor in front of the couch, this won't take long." He waited for the kids to get settled before looking at Emily. "I wanted everyone to hear what I have to say to you," he explained taking a deep breath. "I fell in love with you the first day we met, and since that day, I have loved you more and more, each and every day. There is not a second that goes by, where I don't think about you, miss you, or want to be with you. I do feel the same as you, but just having that feeling is not enough for me, for you, for us, or for Ava." Michael went down on one knee, opened the ring box, asking, "Emily Anderson, will you marry me?"

Emily looked down at, 'The Christmas Teardrop.' "Yes!" she replied happily. "Yes, yes, yes!"

He took the ring out of the box, and as he placed it on her finger, he looked at her and said, "I promise you from this day forward, the only tears you will cry, will be tears of happiness." Then stood, kissed her, and whispered, "I love you, Emily."

"I love you, Michael," she whispered back, "this is one of the happiest days of my life," and then gave him a long passionate kiss. The family waited for them to finish before gathering around to congratulate them. Ava was overjoyed as she hugged her mom and Michael.

Michael stood back and smiled as Emily cheerfully showed off her ring to the young girls and women.

"Let's eat," said Richard pulling the adults towards the kitchen to give Michael and Emily a few moments alone as the children took off into the bedroom.

Emily looked down admiring her ring. "It's so beautiful, and so perfect."

"Like the person wearing it," complimented Michael.

"You say the sweetest things," she replied blushing, "I love you."

"I love you."

They all helped set up the buffet that Michael had prepared. As they ate, they talked about wedding dates, wedding dresses, and the places to have it. About Michael's book being published and Emily's new editor position. After dinner, the children showed off the decorations on 'Grizzly the Christmas Tree,' then one by one, they each stood up and said what they wanted from Santa. It was getting late, and the children needed to get home to their beds, so Michael's family said goodbye and left. While Ava watched television, Michael and Emily cleaned up, and then collapsed together on the couch. Michael put his arm around her as she cuddled into him. Emily thought about the Christmas Eve wish she had made at work, 'I wish to see Michael later on tonight, that we talk, resolve everything, and are together forever,' and suddenly realized it had come true, and that Christmas Eve is truly a magical night were wishes come true.

Chapter 42

They bundled up before leaving Michael's house and Ava walked in the middle, holding her mom and Michael's hand, as they walked down the street. The snow had been falling for a while, and blanketed the ground and the trees, creating an enchanting setting. Once inside Emily's house, Ava ran upstairs to get ready for bed, while Emily poured two glasses of wine and Michael put on the Christmas tree lights and music. Emily and Michael sat closely watching the lights twinkle. Soon after, Ava joined them, kissed each of them on the cheek, then snuggled between them and talked about Santa coming tonight. She asked if Michael knew any Christmas stories. He said he did and told her a funny one about Santa getting stuck in the chimney, and how a young girl named Ava, the elves, and the reindeer tried to get him out, making Ava and her mom laugh. Afterwards, Emily and Michael helped Ava put cookies on a plate for Santa, and carrots on another for the reindeer. She then placed them on the table next to a glass of milk and her Christmas list. Ava said goodnight to Michael with a kiss, then went upstairs with her mom, shortly after Emily joined him.

"Michael, come on," she said motioning with her arm towards her.

"Is everything okay?" he asked walking over to her.

"Everything is fine," Emily replied grinning. "Ava wants both of us to tuck her in," she said grabbing his hand. Together they walked up the stairs, into her room, and tucked her in. Then said goodnight, turned off the light, and went downstairs.

Emily was sipping her wine, watching the lights, and thinking about what had just happened with Ava. "Why don't you stay here, with us?"

"What do you mean?"

"Live here, with Ava and me," she said looking at him, "and make this house our home."

"What about Ava?" he asked apprehensively.

Emily gave him a frown like, 'Are you kidding?' "Ava would love you being here," she said reassuringly.

"I would want her to be okay with it, first," he said needing Ava's reassurance.

"I know what you mean," she said realizing he was right, "I will ask her tomorrow."

"Fair enough," he replied.

"Besides, the last thing you want me to do, is assume," she said laughing.

"Isn't that the truth!" said Michael teasingly.

"Hey, mister," she said with a pouty face.

"But look where it got us," he said cheerfully. "Sometimes things happen for a reason, even not-so-good things."

"I never thought about it that way," she replied joyfully. "It did work out for us in the end, didn't it?"

"It sure did," said Michael lifting his wine glass. 'To us!"

"To us!" repeated Emily touching his glass. She took a sip and looked over at the empty dining room. "You know, you could put your dining room set right in there, it would fit perfectly." She thought some more. "You could put the gas fireplace from your living room right against that wall there…One of your couches and the flat screen television you could put in the basement…and your bedroom set in the spare room…The gas fireplace in your room, up in the attic, along with your other couch, armchair, computer and desk," she said satisfied with her placements. "What do you think?"

"I think you're right," he replied. "You really want me to move in, don't you?"

"I do! I really do!" she said excitedly. "Don't you?"

"I do, and I would in a heartbeat."

She snuggled into him. "That would be a Christmas Day wish come true," she said hoping it was one of Ava's also. She thought for a moment, and wasn't sure whether to ask him or not, then just blurted it out. "Do you want to stay over tonight?"

"I would like that," he replied squeezing her close to him.

"When I say stay over, I meant stay upstairs, with me."

"I know," he replied kissing the top of her head.

"Yay!" she said sitting up. "Then let's finish this wine."

They went upstairs to bed, held each other for a while, started to kiss passionately and made love. Afterwards, Emily cuddled into him. She loved being in his arms. She felt so safe and so secure. Knowing she would feel this way for the rest of her life, she smiled, and drifted off to sleep.

Chapter 43

The door flew open. "It's Christmas morning!" shouted Ava jumping onto the bed.

Emily quickly looked around; Michael was gone. Home again, she thought.

"I thought Michael would be here," said Ava unhappily.

"I thought so too" she replied sadly. "I think he—"

"Here I am," he said walking into the room. "I was just putting on a pot of coffee. I have a feeling it is going to be a long morning of opening presents."

Ava jumped in bed next to her mom. "Come on Michael, lie next to me. Remember I told you every Christmas morning me and Mom snuggle for a bit before we open presents."

"I remembered," he said as he got under the blankets.

Emily now understood why Michael had disappeared.

"This is so much fun," said Ava joyfully.

Ava asking where Michael was and inviting him to snuggle with them was a good sign, thought Emily, and decided now would be as good a time as any to talk to her. "Ava, I am going to ask you something. You don't have to answer me now, you can think about it as long as you want, and if you say no, Michael and I will understand, okay?"

"Okay, Mom," she replied.

"What would you think if Michael, me and you, all lived here together in this house, and made it our home?"

"Like a family?"

"Not like a family...a family," confirmed Emily.

"I love you Santa!" shouted Ava throwing off the blankets and running down the stairs.

Emily looked over at Michael. "Was that a yes?"

"I…don't…know," said Michael slowly.

"Aaaaahhh!" Ava cheerfully screamed from downstairs.

Emily and Michael looked at one another. "She saw the presents."

Ava quickly returned with an envelope in her hand, crawled in the middle of the bed, and lay on her back. "You see it's even been opened, which means Santa read it!" She removed the card and read it out loud as Emily and Michael looked on: "Dear Santa, my Christmas wish is that on Christmas morning I get to snuggle with Mommy and Michael in bed, that Michael lives here with me and Mommy forever, and we are a family, Love Ava, hugs and kisses." She looked at her mom and Michael. "You see, my Christmas Day wish came true, Santa is the best!" she said, as they cuddled together, "I love this Christmas. This is the best Christmas ever."

They went downstairs and opened the presents, and as Ava played on her tablet, they drank their coffees and looked on.

"I wish we could have had Christmas dinner here," confessed Emily, "with both our families."

"That would be nice," replied Michael looking over at her. "Where would we all sit to eat?"

"Well, the storage area by the laundry room contains two long folding tables and sixteen folding chairs. My cousin used them one summer to host something in the backyard," she stated. "She didn't need them, so she left them here in case I ever did," explained Emily then thought for a moment. "The dining room is too small."

"But the attic isn't!" suggested Michael.

"No, it isn't!" she said looking at him excitedly. "That's a great idea!"

"So, what do you think?" asked Michael.

"I think we should," she replied.

"Me too."

"You call your mom, and I will call mine," said Emily.

"Hold on a second," said Michael. "We don't have enough food or drink."

"Michael," said Emily giving him a look, "we'll ask them to bring their dinners and drinks here, between your mom and mine, there will be more than enough."

Michael stood up and took off in a hurry.

"Where are you running off to?" she asked puzzled.

"To call my parents to invite them before you invite yours," he said starting up the stairs.

"Oh no, you don't," she said running after him.

Michael grabbed her phone from the dresser and jumped on the bed. Emily was right behind him and tried to wrestle the phone out of his hand. Out of breath they stopped, looked at each other, then started to kiss passionately. Michael let go of the phone and put his arms around her.

"I love you, Emily."

"I love you, Michael," she replied slowly stretching his arms out. Emily quickly jumped off the bed ran to the bathroom door, turned around, and showed him her phone. "Ha!" she cried, as she leisurely strolled backwards into the bathroom, locking the door behind her.

Michael laughed and shook his head at her trickery.

She came out and lay beside him on the bed. "They'll be here at three. My mom is bringing a big ham, veggies, gravy, dessert, and drinks. She said she had a small turkey as well, but I was thinking your mom would want to bring hers, so I told her to keep it there and eat during the week."

"Yeah, my mom's turkey can feed a small army," said Michael reaching for her phone. "I'll give her a call."

Emily pulled away. "Do you mind asking your family to come for three thirty?" she asked. "I want us to have some time with mine and to tell them about this," she said lifting up her ring.

"Not at all," he replied giving her a kiss.

"Here," she said passing it to him, "my pin is two, four, eight, six, two."

Michael called his mom. "You're going to bring, turkey, sides, dessert, wine, and beer," he reconfirmed. "Yes, we need dishes and cutlery," he replied. "That would be great, come around four," he verified. "Okay, see you then, bye."

"Four?" she asked.

"You need more than thirty minutes,"

"Thank you," she said kissing him fondly, "you're the best."

They went to the basement, brought up the tables and chairs, and set them up in the attic. After cleaning them, Emily put down white tablecloths, while Michael hung Christmas decorations and lights around the windows. Finished, they stood arm in arm admiring their accomplishment.

"This room looks so festive and charming. This dinner is going to be so special," she said happily, as she rested her head on his shoulder.

Emily's parents and sister arrived at three. They took their food into the kitchen, gave them a drink, and then sat them down in the living room while Emily and Michael stood in front of them. "Mom, Dad, Debbie I have wonderful news…Michael and I are engaged!" she said flashing her ring.

Her family leapt off the couch, hugging and kissing them both.

"Let me see that ring?" asked her mom. "It's absolutely gorgeous!"

"It's the most beautiful ring I've ever seen," sighed Debbie.

"It a family heirloom from his great-aunt Carol, it's called 'The Christmas Teardrop," she explained to them.

"I love that name, and I'm so happy for you both," said Debbie who started to weep, which made Emily, then her mom cry.

"Another drink, John," asked Michael as they left for the kitchen. "Emily is a wonderful girl, and I am a lucky man."

"Isabelle and I know we don't have to say to you, take care of her, because we already know you will," he said looking over at his daughter. "Look how happy she is, she's glowing."

When they went back into the living room Emily asked for everyone's attention. "There is more!" she said pulling Michael close to her. "Tell them," she said excitedly.

"On Friday, I found out my book will be getting published in the new year," he said modestly.

"Congratulations," said John as he shook his hand, while Isabelle and Debbie hugged him.

"Wait! There is more," he said proudly looking over at Emily.

"You are now looking at the new editor for Peter Paterson Publishers of New York," she said elatedly.

After they hugged and kissed her, she explained how she got offered the position.

"It's well deserved," praised Michael.

"Here, here," agreed John.

When Michael's family arrived, they were introduced, and they talked for a while before placing the settings, warming up the food, and putting it on the table. After everyone took their seats, the wine was poured.

Emily noticed something. "Michael, we have one too many settings," she said as everyone looked at the empty chair, then him. Suddenly his phone went off.

"Give me one minute," he said as he went downstairs.

When he came back Emily looked over at him and was about to ask him about the extra setting again until he moved out of the way. "Sue!" Emily yelled running over to her. "What are you doing here?"

"Michael sent a text asking me to drop in for dinner. He said there was something you needed to tell me and that it couldn't wait till our next coffee chat," replied Sue looking her up and down. "You seem fine to me, in fact, you look radiant."

Emily showed Sue the ring.

Sue screamed as they both jumped up and down. Then Sue squeezed her tightly and looked over at Michael saying, "get over here you," and squeezed him too.

Emily introduced everyone to Sue, after she sat, Emily grabbed Michael's hand then asked Ava to join them. The three of them stood there as everyone looked on. Emily spoke. "I would like to thank Michael's family, my family, and my friend Sue, for celebrating this special

Christmas dinner with my family, me, Ava, and Michael, thank you." Everyone clapped and cheered, and did so again, when Emily and Michael kissed.

Once they sat down, Ava said grace, and they ate their family Christmas dinner.

After everyone had gone home, and Ava was fast asleep in her bed, Emily and Michael lay on theirs holding one another.

"This was my best Christmas ever," revealed Emily.

"Mine too," Michael concurred as they cuddled in silence for a while. "You know I read your short stories."

"You did? What did you think of them?"

"I thought they were very good."

"Really?"

"I think you should put them all together as a collection of short stories."

"Maybe I will," replied Emily considering it, "but do you know what I would like to do first?"

"What's that?" he asked interestedly.

"I would like you and me to write a story together."

"A collaboration?" he asked.

"Yes, a collaboration."

"Do you have any ideas about what?"

It should be a magical Christmas story full of wishes, dreams, and hopes…about caring, sharing, giving, love and support…and it should revolve around a couple falling in love and take place in a small, snowy town like Aurora…And it has to begin with a heated and hurtful, relationship-ending argument, like the one we had, then go back to the first day we met."

"I like it," said Michael with a smile. "Do you have a title for it?"

"I do!" replied Emily happily.

"What?" asked Michael curiously.

"The Christmas Teardrop."